"If what I've heard is true, you want to launch this charity for children. But no one trusts you to be involved in *anything* concerning children. Because, let's face it, who would have *you* spearheading a charity for *children*? You are, by all accounts, cantankerous, ill-tempered, foul-mouthed and hot-headed. Did I miss anything?"

Dmitri took a step toward her and took a great amount of satisfaction in watching her shrink a bit. "Yes. I'm also something of a womaniser. That doesn't help my cause. I mean, what with all the rumors flying around about how I meet a woman, take her to dinner and have her naked, between my sheets and screaming my name in only a couple of hours—"

Victoria held up a hand, clearly irritated with the line of dialogue. "I could solve your problems," she said, twisting the subject expertly.

"By marrying me?"

"I wouldn't actually have to *marry* you. I would simply need to hang on your arm for a while, then wear your ring for a while after that. Long enough to get things going."

"You have thought this through." And she had ambushed him, with no warning at all. A smart woman. Were she a burly man and not a fine-boned female she might have made an excellent fighter.

A wo

But if  she would

Maisey Yates is the *USA TODAY* bestselling author of more than thirty romance novels. She has a coffee habit she has no interest in kicking, and a slight Pinterest addiction. She lives with her husband and children in the Pacific Northwest. When Maisey isn't writing she can be found singing in the grocery store, shopping for shoes online, and probably not doing dishes. Check out her website: www.maiseyyates.com

Visit the author profile page at millsandboon.co.uk for more titles

HIS DIAMOND
OF CONVENIENCE

BY
MAISEY YATES

MILLS
BOON

Published in Great Britain 2015
by Mills & Boon, an imprint of Harlequin (UK) Limited,
Eton House, 18-24 Paradise Road, Richmond, Surrey, TW9 1SR

Harlequin's policy is to use papers that are natural,
renewable and recyclable products and made from wood grown in
sustainable forests. The logging and manufacturing processes conform
to the legal environmental regulations of the country of origin.

Printed and bound in Spain
by

HIS DIAMOND
OF CONVENIENCE

For Pippa,
because you've loved Victoria since she first appeared.
Thank you for all of your support, now and always.

CHAPTER ONE

VICTORIA INTENSELY DISLIKED places like this. Gyms with boxing rings, hanging punching bags and various other accoutrements. The lighting was dim, casting everything in a dull shadow. It was probably for the best, all things considered, else it might reveal the stains from dirt, blood and whatever else that undoubtedly lingered on the canvas. The air smelled of sweat, of testosterone. And she could truly think of nothing less appealing.

The entire place, and all of its inhabitants, needed to be hosed down.

If it wasn't absolutely necessary she find Dmitri Markin, she would never have stepped foot in here.

She ran her hand over her hair, checking to see that everything was still in place, then walked forward, her high heels loud on the concrete floor as she strode through the workout area, studiously ignoring the male gazes that were following her progress through the room.

These were not the male gazes she was looking for. And therefore, she was uninterested.

Oily muscles did nothing for her. Thank you very much.

Not unless she needed a heavy box lifted. Then oily muscles could certainly serve a purpose, but not aesthetically. Not in her world.

One of the men she walked past whistled and she felt her muscles tense, starting at the base of her skull and spreading downward, her shoulders bunching up as the tension bled outward.

She didn't give the man the satisfaction of pausing, neither did she look at him. Rather, she ratcheted her chin up a notch and forged ahead, tightening her hold on her purse and keeping her strides even.

Over the years she had become something of a challenge to men. They knew she had a reputation for keeping herself separate, for keeping herself distant. And that made her a temptation, apparently, which was just one more reason she had to disdain the gender. Which was potentially unfair of her, but she didn't care.

In the interest of maintaining the family peace and getting back in her father's good books, she had at one time entertained the idea of making a suitable marriage. And in her mind, and the mind of her father, a suitable marriage meant marriage to royalty. Yet it had failed spectacularly. Because when she had managed to secure herself a royal fiancé, he had gone on to fall in love with their matchmaker.

Which had put her back at square one. Focusing on her charities and on raising her family's profile in the media.

Until she had found out that Dmitri Markin had something she wanted. And that he wanted something she had.

Now she had a whole new plan for fixing the pain she caused her family. And it would be a whole lot better than marrying a prince. Assuming she could accomplish it. And she would. Because she didn't fail. Not anymore.

She had the chance to atone for past sins. She'd spotted this open door, so she was walking through it.

Right at the moment she was thinking of metaphorical doors, she walked through a literal door and into the back of the gym. This was a private training room, so she had been told when she had inquired about Dmitri's haunts. And just as she had been informed, by the curvaceous redhead she had met at a party earlier in the week, Dmitri was here, grappling with another man.

They were both shirtless, in black pants, fighting as if their lives depended on it. She sniffed. Silly. Their lives certainly did not depend on it.

Men.

She recognized Dmitri immediately. He was larger than his opponent, well muscled and sporting an armful of ink. She didn't know what the symbols were, or what they represented; she only knew that, were the tabloids to be believed, they were the sort of thing that caused a lot of women to swoon.

Not her. She was not given to swooning.

To her, they were merely beneficial because they helped her to identify her target sooner.

She stopped walking, crossing her arms beneath her breasts and cocking her hip to the right. "Dmitri Markin?"

He wrapped his arms around his partner's waist, bent and flipped the other man over his shoulder, letting him land flat on his back on the mats. Then Dmitri straightened and turned to face her, hands on his lean hips, his chest pitching with the effort of his breathing. Sweat rolled down his skin, skating over his ab muscles and drawing her eye toward the waistband of his shorts. Toward the line of hair that continued down farther beneath the fabric.

Heat assaulted her and she redirected her gaze quickly. And that didn't help at all, because as distracting as his body was, well, his face wasn't any better.

A ripple of unease went through her. Photographs hadn't prepared her for the sheer magnetism he presented. An element she hadn't accounted for.

The realization made her stomach squeeze tight, apprehension winding through her. She was momentarily shocked, turned to stone, by the man standing before her.

Considering what he'd done for a living it wouldn't be outside the norm for his face to be a living record of every punch he'd taken. A time line of his years spent in the ring. But no. He didn't have the decency to be deformed. His dark hair was rumpled in a near-stylish manner, dark eyes glimmering with humor. His nose had a bump in it, likely from being broken, and it only made him look…rakish, not disfigured. How annoying. Then there was the deep groove in his upper lip, likely a badly healed split, so that his mouth gave the impression he was always sneering slightly, even when he was smiling. That was rakish, too.

A shiver ran through her and she fought to keep from showing the evidence of it on her face. She needed to secure this deal. So that the rift between her and her father could be stitched back together. So that she could finally move on with her life.

She couldn't afford to be distracted. Not when she was so close.

Damn the man. Was there nowhere she could look? She let her eyes drift back to his chest, and she felt her cheeks get warmer. She had no idea what was going on with her, why for an instant she had felt frozen. Why she was unable to tear her eyes away from his body.

Perhaps it was simple appreciation at the weapon he clearly was. His past was no secret; everyone was well aware of his work as a mixed martial arts fighter. And even though it had been nearly a decade since he'd set foot into a ring, he was obviously still keeping himself honed.

So yes, it had something to do with all of that. And she was moving on.

"I am he." He took his hands from his hips and rolled his shoulders backward, thrusting his chest forward as he stretched his muscles, the shift and bunch of the lines on his body capturing her attention yet again. These were the very glistening muscles she had just been disavowing and dismissing, claiming they could not be aesthetically pleasing. At the moment she had to admit there was *some* aesthetic appeal.

Though, it wasn't in the way women typically admired men. No. Not in the least. This was artistic admiration. She had an eye for clean lines, good design. Dmitri was like fine architecture.

She cleared her throat. "My name is Victoria. Victoria Calder."

"I do not recall hearing your name before. I don't think we have an appointment." His every word was just slightly flat, still colored by a hint of Russian accent, though it was faded after long years of living in the UK. "Unless," he said, a slow smile crossing his lips, "you are looking for a chance to challenge me on the mats."

She gripped the strap of her purse tighter. "That's quite funny. Do you often have women coming to *challenge you on the mats*?"

The smile broadened, turned wicked, and her stomach turned over, twisted. She gritted her teeth and fought to maintain her composure. "More often than you might think."

She cleared her throat. "Excellent. Charming. That is, however, not why I'm here."

"Well, if it is legitimate business, an appointment is typically made." He looked her over, his gaze leaving a trail of heat behind. She tried to get her focus back. Tried to recite her plan in her head. Envision her goal. She could not be deterred. "There is a certain type of woman who shows up unannounced. If you have legitimate business I suggest you call my secretary and make an appointment. Otherwise, take off your dress."

She ignored the rough command. She also ignored the

rush of heat that came along with it. He was expecting her to get all flustered. She was certain. And she would not give him the satisfaction. At least, she wouldn't show it, but the wild thumping of her heart made her think *flustered* was exactly what she was whether she wanted to be or not.

She swallowed hard and met his eyes. "I'll keep the dress on, thanks. Shall we adjourn to a more comfortable setting?"

"I am perfectly comfortable. And I was not expecting to have a meeting. Therefore, *I* will stay here."

The man he had been fighting had risen to his feet now and was standing there looking at the two of them. "Then perhaps you might ask him to leave," Victoria said.

"Because you're going to take the dress off?"

She cleared her throat, schooling her expression into one of disdain, ignoring the prickling feeling on the back of her neck. "Sadly for you, no. You can let go of that fantasy quickly. The dress isn't coming off until I get home and step into a nice warm bath, which, after the harassment I've endured today, is well deserved. I'm staying dressed. And we need to have a discussion."

"It sounds like I might be in trouble. But I have never slept with you, so I don't see why I should be. I have not caused you any trouble. Yet."

She gritted her teeth. He was really pulling out all the stops. Fortunately it was nothing she hadn't dealt with before. Typically the man wasn't shirtless. Typically he was not quite so good-looking. But neither of those things mattered, not to her. "Either he goes or I go," she said, keeping her tone bored. "And I have a feeling you want to hear what I have to say."

Dmitri cocked his head to the side, a small smile curving one side of his mouth. "Nigel, leave us for moment."

The other man nodded and walked out. Then Dmitri turned his focus to her. "Speak."

She readjusted her hold on her bag, her palms feeling sweaty now. "I am not a dog, nor indeed am I any type of pet. Rephrase."

He chuckled, a dark sound that poured over her like melting honey. That made her shiver. "Okay, why don't you tell me what you came here to tell me so that I can go take my shower?"

Her patience was wearing thin. She was still standing in the sweaty gym and, frankly, his bare chest was having more of an effect on her than she would like. Was making her feel as if there was a gaping hole in her plan. All of that was conspiring to put her in a very cranky mood. And that was the only thing that could account for the words that came out of her mouth next.

"All right, Mr. Markin. I just came here to ask you a question. Will you marry me?"

Dmitri looked at the powerhouse blonde standing in front of him. She was pale, with slim curves, long, lean legs and an expression that could make a lesser man wilt where he stood. And if the look of her didn't accomplish it, that crisp English accent, so posh it made a man feel as if he ought to put on a tie before he could speak to her, would.

He, however, was not a lesser man and was therefore not wilting. Not in the least. And he wasn't putting on a damned tie.

"Sorry, you might have had better luck with the proposal if you had taken the dress off."

"Cheap thrills are your thing, then?" she asked, arching a finely shaped brow.

He crossed his arms over his chest. "Yeah. I like a cheap thrill. Though, these days I can afford an expensive thrill, too. But honestly, why not just embrace every thrill available?" He looked her over again, taking in every curved line, every enticingly female part of her. "I would have picked you for an expensive thrill. But as you've price checked yourself…"

"You'll find me short on thrills, Mr. Markin," she said, her voice biting. "Unless what I have to offer you is a thrill—and do not get too excited. It has nothing to do with bare skin."

"Marriage usually does have something to do with bare skin. It is the only reason I can see anyone would enter into the union. Though, I've found my share outside of it."

"Which could be part of why you're having such a hard time finding support for your charity."

The back of his neck prickled. "How did you know about that?"

The charity he was working on establishing in Colvin's name was not common knowledge. Yes, he'd approached a few people about it, but he'd told those people to be discreet. The reactions had all been the same, too.

He would need support. Because a man with a reputation for driving too fast, sleeping with too many women, a man who had earned his fortune in the ring…would have his efforts met with cynicism.

And he could not afford to have a negative reaction. Colvin was dead. There would be no paying him back in this life. But he could show the world what the other man had done for him. Offer choices to children who were in the position he had once been in.

Choices he had never had. Control that had been wrenched from him on a cold day in Moscow.

"I always have an ear to the ground," Victoria said, "plus, I have sat on the board for a great many charities over the years and have quite a few connections. I use those connections to my advantage."

"How does supporting a kids' charity benefit you?"

She blinked wide blue eyes slowly. "What do you mean? I'm only thinking of the children."

He swore crudely in Russian and laughed. "Right. I'm sure you are."

"I take it you don't believe me?"

"Do I believe the Ice Princess is thinking of the children? No. You would have to emanate *some* warmth before I would believe that."

She let out an exasperated sigh. "Sorry. Too busy to emanate today I'm afraid. Perhaps another time. However, I assure you I approach my charity work with complete dedication. But I save my passion for my work, so none for you, I'm afraid. Now, about my proposal…"

"*Why* did you propose?"

She lifted a brow. "It was love at first sight?"

"No."

She leveled her gaze, meeting his, her eyes alight with determination. "I want London Diva back."

He frowned at the mention of one of his holdings. "Excuse me?"

"London Diva. I want the company signed back over to my family."

"Calder," he said, repeating her name. Of course he hadn't made the immediate connection. He'd bought the chain of high-end retail stores out from under Nathan Barrett a few years back, but he knew it had been founded by Geoffrey Calder some thirty years earlier. "You're Geoffrey Calder's… Well, you can't be his wife because you just proposed to me. His daughter?"

"Very good guess. A correct guess."

"So, you walk in and propose marriage, then demand

a portion of my business. And what will you do for me in return?"

"You may have seen some of my charity work in the media. They speak quite highly of me. Some outlets have made comparisons with Mother Teresa, though I think that's selling her a bit short. It isn't as if I've given up all of my worldly possessions," she said, flashing her expensive-looking handbag. "But, though I'm not a paragon, I am, compared to you. And I have something you want. Something you seem incapable of buying."

He waved a hand. "Foolish woman. I have yet to find anything I can't buy."

"Except a better reputation." The expression on her face was almost comically angelic. He imagined she would look innocent of a crime just as she was about to cut a man's throat.

He liked that.

But what he didn't like was the fact that she had his balls in a vise. And was tightening it slowly. His reputation as a businessman was flawless. His reputation as a human being had some issues. "And why do you suppose I need to improve my reputation?"

"Because if what I've heard is true, you want to launch this charity for children. Gyms offering free and reduced-rate lessons in martial arts and other physical fitness activities for children in high risk situations. But no one trusts you to be involved in anything concerning children. Because let's face it, who would have *you* spearheading a charity for *children.* You are, by all accounts, cantankerous, ill-tempered, foulmouthed and hotheaded. Did I miss anything?"

He took a step toward her and took a great amount of satisfaction in watching her shrink a bit. "Yes. I'm also something of a womanizer. That doesn't help my cause. I mean, what with all the rumors flying around about how I meet a woman, take her to dinner and have her naked, between my sheets and screaming my name in only a couple of hours—"

She held up a hand, clearly irritated with the line of dialogue. Good. "That's only the tip of the iceberg, though, isn't it? Drunk driving. Fraternizing with married women. Many of whom are *mothers*. You certainly don't have a history of caring if you tear families apart."

Dmitri bristled at her blatant reference to his most recent scandal. "Lavinia left out some critical information when I took her to bed."

"That she was married?"

"Oh, hell no. I don't care about that. I'm not the one who made vows. But I did not know she had children."

In many ways, he preferred conducting his affairs with women who had other attachments. It allowed him as much detachment as he wanted. Which was essential. He didn't have relationships, he had sex.

He didn't sleep with his lovers. That required trust, and he didn't trust the women he had affairs with.

But that was because he didn't trust anyone.

Victoria made a disgusted sound in the back of her throat. "Yes. Well. In that case you're practically a saint, aren't you?"

"The patron saint of vodka and orgasms, maybe."

Color flooded Victoria's cheeks. "Odd. I've never seen you depicted on the stained glass at mass."

"Something to do with my excommunication I'm sure," he said drily.

"I could solve your problems," she said, twisting the subject expertly.

"By marrying me?"

She chuckled, the sound like a fork on crystal. "Don't

be stupid. I wouldn't actually have to *marry* you. I would simply need to hang on your arm for a while, then wear your ring for a while after that. Long enough to get things going."

"You have thought this through." And she had ambushed him with no warning at all. A smart woman. Were she a burly man and not a fine-boned female she might have made an excellent fighter.

A worthy opponent.

But she was not a fighter, and not his opponent. And was, in this moment, mainly irritating.

"Of course I have. I was hardly going to storm in here without a plan," she said, her tone dripping with disdain.

Just for that, he would make her pay. He was not beneath her. Her or anyone else. And he would not allow her to speak to him as if he was.

"Well, sadly for you, you don't know my schedule all that well. I have somewhere to be soon, and that means I need to go back to my place, shower and change."

"Well…where is that?"

"Happily for you, just upstairs." He had a set of apartments above the gym, an odd choice, he knew. This gym wasn't in the trendy part of town, but it was where he'd got his start when he'd come from Russia to London and it held sentimental value to him.

Even more now that Colvin was dead. The loss of his mentor was a heavy weight around his neck, and being here made him feel…well, like the old man wasn't entirely gone.

Fanciful garbage he wasn't normally given to, but he hadn't been able to let go of this place.

Colvin had given him choices again. Colvin had given him—not his old life back—but a new life. One that consisted of more than grubby bars, threadbare blankets and foam mattresses on cement floors. One that consisted of more than taking blow after blow, washing the blood off in a dirty bathroom in the back of an underground club and going back for more…

Choice was what Colvin had given him. It was what Dmitri wanted to give to the children who would benefit from the charity.

It was what Victoria Calder was slowly tightening her grasp on, and tugging away from him, as she laid out a finely honed argument that showed him two options. Her, or failure. Dishonor or death.

Much like being back on the streets of Moscow.

It made anger fire straight through his blood, a wall of flame that heated him from the inside out. But he would never let her see that.

He knew better than to expose his weaknesses to his opponent.

"You want me to come upstairs while you shower?" she asked, obviously incredulous. Good.

"Unless it's a problem."

She sputtered and shook her head. "Oh no. No. Why would it be a problem? Of course it isn't a problem. You just…lead the way, then." She waved a manicured hand and he fought the urge to do something shocking. Grab it. Tug her to him. Wrap an arm around her waist and hold her against him. Prove he wasn't some lackey she could come in and order around.

Because no one had informed Victoria Calder that not everyone leaped to attention at the sound of her crisp accent. He, however, would not. And she would learn quickly.

But damn her for finding a weak point. He was not given to emotional connections. He had one. And she had found it.

"Right this way, then," he said, not bothering to look at her as he forged through the workout room and to a door that was nearly hidden in the back. He entered in his code on the keypad on the door and he heard the lock give, then he jerked the door open, holding it. "After you, Ms. Calder."

She shot him a look he was certain was intended to be deadly, but he continued on anyway.

"You will find I am not wounded by icy glares, Ms. Calder," he said.

Her back stiffened and she stopped midstride.

"I am not trying to wound you," she said. "That runs counter to my objective."

"Of marrying me. Yes. It would not do for you to become a widow before we get a chance to start our new, charitable life together."

She sniffed audibly. "Indeed." She started walking again, her high heels clicking on the hard floor.

He forced a chuckle and followed her up the stairs, his eyes pinned to her shapely ass. For now, he wouldn't focus on the feeling of entrapment that was winding itself around his throat. He would focus on her skirt. That pencil skirt she was wearing was a gift. He'd rarely appreciated what well-cut, high-class clothes could do when fitted just right to a woman's curves. He typically aimed for obvious targets, not hidden gems like this one.

Right now he was rethinking that.

Then she paused and turned to him again, one pale brow arched, and he immediately remembered why, in spite of how lovely their asses looked in pencil skirts, he didn't go for women like her.

He liked a good time. He liked a simple time.

Work was hard. Life was hard. Sex, in his opinion, should be easy.

And nothing about Victoria Calder said *easy*.

"Did you have something else to say, Ms. Calder?" he asked.

She pinched her lips together. "No." Then she turned and continued on up the stairs.

She stopped in front of the closed door at the top of the staircase, her hands clasped in front of her, fingers curled around the strap of the bag she seemed so proud of.

He positioned himself behind her very purposefully and leaned in, reaching past her to the keypad on the wall, entering a different code from the one he had put in outside. He could feel her indrawn breath, could see the way that it caused her shoulders to rise, then stiffen. He felt a smile curve his lips as he lingered, his fingers still hovering over the buttons after he had finished entering the code, taking a pause before he opened the door.

He didn't like being surprised. He liked even less the thought that this woman might think she could come into his facility and start issuing demands. He was not a dog waiting to be brought to heel, and she would realize that soon enough.

The power was his. Even if he was intrigued by the idea of making use of her and her offer, it did not mean that she had the upper hand. She had already revealed that she had more at stake than he did, and he was prepared to use that against her.

Because no matter that Dmitri Markin had long ago left the ring, he was a fighter. And everyone who entered his territory was an opponent as far as he was concerned. Victoria was no different. He would not hesitate to find her weaknesses so that in future, if need be, he could exploit them.

"After you," he said, keeping his hand firmly braced on the door, holding it open.

Victoria didn't look at him; rather she walked straight

ahead and into the room. She was an icy creature, and prideful. It intrigued him. It also provided him with a weakness. She prized her control—that much was clear. It was connected to her pride—that much was also clear. And now he had found her pressure point.

He walked in the room after her, closing the door behind him. It was a sparse room, but much more upscale than one typically anticipated after seeing the gym below. He'd had it remodeled a year or so ago as a place where he could go and be free from the press. Free from any ex-flames. Free of any expectation. That was what the gym had always been for him.

No one bothered him here. At least until Victoria Calder had showed up.

Victoria continued more deeply into the room, her high heels clicking on the high-gloss black tile. She was looking around, likely thinking the same thing he'd been observing. That this room was not what one would expect upon entry to the gym. Clean lines, modern furniture, black, white and stainless steel everywhere. No windows. He was buried too deeply within the gym. And he found he liked it that way. A way to truly be cut off from the outside world, something he'd lacked in his teenage years.

He pushed open the bathroom door. "I'll only be a few minutes." He walked inside and stripped off his clothes, not bothering to close the door behind him as he moved to turn the shower on.

If Victoria wanted to beard the lion in his den, she would have to accept the consequences.

CHAPTER TWO

HE HADN'T CLOSED the door. Victoria stood in the middle of Dmitri's spotless, ultramodern apartment, still holding on to her purse as if it was a lifeline, not quite certain of what to do next.

She could hear the water running, assumed that he was now in the shower.

And he had not closed the door.

He was naked. Wet.

It was inappropriate.

And very likely, all a part of him trying to get the upper hand. His behavior absolutely reeked of that. And she was determined that she wouldn't let it work. She did not respond to intimidation tactics. No matter what form they took. There was no doubt in her mind that this was, in fact, an attempt at intimidating her. Too bad for him it wouldn't work. A little bit of wobble in her knees wasn't going to put her off.

But while she might not be intimidated, she *was* a little bit uncomfortable. Because her mind kept going back to *naked* and *wet*. Which was unusual. More than unusual, it was almost unheard of. She'd been cured of base lust very early on. Once she'd realized how it could be used to manipulate, it had lost its luster.

She let out a heavy breath, feeling exasperated at the turn this had taken. Not that she had expected him to accept her proposal on sight. But she hadn't expected all this, either.

She was determined to play it cool, determined that she would not allow him to put her on her back foot.

And just as she had made the resolution firm, it broke apart like a sand castle being hit by a wave. Because just then Dmitri reappeared, water droplets rolling down his chest, a towel wrapped around his hips. If she had been paying attention and not been so busy gathering her determination, she might have realized that he'd turned the water off. But she hadn't. And he had. And he had managed to surprise her again. Of course, she wouldn't let him see that.

She swallowed hard, her throat parched. Which was odd since he was…wet.

"Do you own a shirt, Mr. Markin?" She looked him up and down, doing her best to keep her expression disinterested. "Because I have yet see evidence of it."

"I do, but I don't always see occasion to wear one. Does it bother you?"

"Not at all. I was merely concerned. You are a billionaire, so obviously I assumed that you were more than able to cover the expenses in your life. But if not, I'm happy to take up a collection. Charity is after all my area of expertise."

He chuckled, the sound dark and rich, and far more offputting than she would like to admit. "Your concern is very touching. However, you should not worry yourself with my clothing needs, as I find they are adequately met. But you do seem to know one thing I am in want of, and that is a better public image. I am wondering who your sources are."

Victoria tapped her chin. "A lady never tells. Anyway, don't worry too much about it. Your part in this will be minimal, all told. As I said, we won't even really have to get married."

"I only need to buy you a ring, is that it?"

She arched a brow. "If the implication is that I might be doing this to get a piece of jewelry out of you, then allow me to inform you that you're very wrong. I have my own money, Mr. Markin, and I'm not in need of yours. I could buy my own damned ring." She said the words crisply, knowing that she was betraying her annoyance.

After the loss of London Diva her father had withdrawn his support—both emotionally and financially. Her mother had left so long ago Victoria could barely remember her, but it hadn't mattered because she'd had her father. She'd been the center of his world. And then…it was as though a veil had been torn from his eyes and he'd seen her, not as his princess, but as a flawed, craven creature, who wasn't even related to the little girl he'd once cherished.

Oh, he hadn't stopped speaking to her. Hadn't thrown her out of the house, or openly shamed her. But the disapproval that always hung in the air was palpable.

So, she'd learned to be independent.

She had access to her trust fund. She'd made her own investments with it, paid back the fund and now proudly lived predominantly with her own money.

The break from her family had been what prompted her to get involved in charity work. Initially as an outward show of some sort of virtue, but in the end, it had come to mean a lot more to her than that.

It had taught her the value of independence. Of hard work. It was the one place she could see positive change coming out of her actions. A positive change that helped others. A much-needed outlet when, at home, she was still paying for mistakes of the past.

Not for much longer.

"You want your family business back. I don't see any point in skirting around the real reason you're here."

"Yes, nothing more complicated than that. Nothing

more nefarious than that. It's such a small portion of your empire I fail to see why it would be of concern to you. I want my birthright, my inheritance."

He said nothing, his dark eyes fixed on her as though he was waiting for more. So she obliged him. "Like I said, a straightforward transaction. My family's company is returned to me at the end of our agreement, and I will do everything in my power to ensure that your reputation is solid. With me helping in the establishment of your charity you should have benefactors throwing money at you from all corners of the earth. I guarantee you that my presence in your life will improve your standing in the media."

"You are quite confident in yourself."

Victoria tried her best to keep her eyes on his…and not on his chest. "I see no point in failing to acknowledge your strengths. I know mine. Shallow, some might call them, or unimportant. But I see them for what they are. I have spent much of my life learning to be a savvy investor, and also donating my time to worthy causes. My reputation is flawless." She hesitated. "I was very nearly engaged to a prince about three years ago. So that does make for interesting commentary on my past. However, if there was any dirt to be discovered about me, it would have been discovered then. Around the time I was with Stavros the media became quite interested in me, and since there were no scandals then…"

"There won't be one now. Unless… Why did your engagement with the prince fail?" It was his turn to smile. "Or did he have a similar deal to me?"

"Nothing like that. I intended to marry Stavros. Sadly, he fell in love with someone else. And I wished him the best when it happened. I made not a ripple in the waves of the media when things ended between us. I was nothing but gracious."

He crossed his arms over his broad chest, the muscles in his forearms flexing, distracting her yet again. Her eyes followed the dark lines of the tattoos that were inked into his skin, and to the leather band that was tied around his wrist. He was so very different than the kind of men she typically interacted with. Different and fascinating.

"Yes, you do come over as very gracious."

She nodded in agreement, even though she knew he was being sarcastic.

He uncrossed his arms and waved a hand, beginning to pace around the room. And she was very worried for the precarious position of the towel, riding so low on his hips. Okay, maybe *worried* wasn't the appropriate word. *Concerned? Fascinated.* No, she should not be fascinated. She knew better than to be fascinated by men.

"How long do you think this will take?" he asked.

She blinked, almost unable to believe that he sounded interested. "We'll need to put in several appearances together. We will need to organize a few galas, where we will collect pledges and let the public know about what you hope to accomplish. We will need to make contact with the appropriate people in high society, and if not in high society per se, those who are part of the one percent. That takes time. In all actuality I'm imagining we will need somewhere around three months to accomplish all of this."

"A month is a more acceptable time frame."

Victoria tried to imagine planning something on the scale she was picturing in only thirty days. Obviously the man hadn't planned many parties. "Yes, but sometimes no matter how liberally you throw money at things time is still a factor. It's unforgiving, really."

"You've got that right. Time really is quite unforgiving."

Ironic to hear him say that, since time had clearly been good to him. In his thirties, Dmitri was in peak physical condition, and for a man who had lived the kind of life that he had, he was strikingly devoid of scars.

"I can't promise it will be a success," she said, pressing on. "You know I have to allow for variables. I'm not entirely certain what all *your* past entails, and that might hinder both of us."

"I do not expect a guarantee—what I expect is effort."

She shrugged, feigning a casualness she did not feel at all. "As long as you understand that while I can make a silk purse out of a sow's ear I will have a harder time making one out of a horse's ass."

He laughed again, his dark chuckle filling the space. "You are amusing—I will grant you that."

"I am gleeful at the thought of being a source of your amusement." She was not gleeful, not by half. Her heart was racing, the thrill of possible victory pouring through her. Yes, this must be what it was like to be an opponent on the mats. No, she had not defeated him with her fists, but persuading someone using only her tongue was much more satisfying. "Anyway, I promise I will keep my cleverness under control when we're in public venues."

"Don't. I hardly think the press would be impressed by my engagement to a simpering, unclever female. Moreover, I doubt they would believe it. I like a fight. I like a fight in the ring, I like a fight in the boardroom. And I very much like a fight in the bedroom."

His words sent a flash of heat through her. And they echoed what she had just been thinking moments ago, minus the commentary about the bedroom, so closely in fact she feared for a second he might be a mind reader. Which would be bad indeed, since she had spent an undue amount of time pondering his muscles.

"And what kind of woman do you suppose the press might expect you to be with?"

He began to pace again. "When I choose opponents in the ring I choose them because I know they're going to give me a good match. I like someone who is clever, strong and fast. I like someone who will make me believe I might lose, if only for a moment. I like a challenge," he said, his voice rough, sending a shiver through her. "So just be yourself. That should be enough."

In spite of herself, Victoria felt strangely complimented. But she wouldn't let him see it. In fact, now that she was aware of it, she wouldn't let herself feel it. She only needed the approval of one person, the *forgiveness* of one person, and that was her father.

Sixteen years of perfection erased by one mistake. And every year since desperately trying to regain it.

Her father was the only one who could absolve her.

"I can be myself, Mr. Markin. Effortlessly, as I imagine most people can, but the question is which version of myself would you like?"

His smile turned feral. "Do most people have more than one version of themselves, Ms. Calder?"

"Everyone does."

"Not everyone," he said, his deep voice rolling over her in a wave. "Everything that you see now is all that I am. This apartment, this gym, my work. I have been other things—I have been a great many other things. But this is all that's left."

"I'm not sure I believe that." There was something strangely grim about that. And there was something about it that she couldn't quite believe, either. For some reason, though, she believed that he bought into it wholly and completely. And she was not certain why.

He seemed to think that he had only one layer, that this was the sum total of what he was, as though you could leave versions of yourself behind like an exoskeleton. Victoria knew better. Victoria knew that the part of herself that had betrayed her family still existed. She knew it, and that was why she kept it squashed. Forgetting what you were capable of doing didn't do anyone any favors.

And she was capable of great stupidity.

She wondered why it was Dmitri Markin thought he had defeated his old demons entirely. Then she wondered if somehow he had. And for a moment she envied him. Because she would never be free of those past versions of herself. All she could do was try to atone for them.

"I know there are all sorts of people who believe in past lives," he said, "who believe that when we die we are reincarnated as someone or something else. I'm not sure about that. But I do know that sometimes things in this life change you, burn you, leave everything you were as nothing more than ashes at your feet. And when that happens, you have no choice but to walk forward into a new life. Whether you want to or not."

"That sounds…bleak."

"Perhaps. But I've had many changes since then. All to do with Colvin. And the reason this charity is so important to me. Thanks to him, I am not the man I was."

"Who were you?" she asked.

"A very bad man," he said. His words sent a shiver through her, down her spine and to her feet.

"And now you're a good man?" she asked, her voice thinner than she'd like it to be.

"I wouldn't say that. But not as dangerous."

Her heart bumped hard against her chest. "You were dangerous?"

He did nothing more than flash a smile, and this time she was certain she saw a predatory edge to it. "I find it best to leave the past buried."

Something about the way he said this sent trail of ice

down to the pit of her stomach, making her shiver, causing goose bumps to break out on her arms.

"So…I suppose we should finalize things. I have other
appointments." She was suddenly very aware of the fact that
he was still standing there in a towel, and even more aware
of the fact that somewhere over the past couple of minutes
she had forgotten. She would love to feel triumphant about
that, love to feel triumphant about the fact that she had obviously mastered whatever thing was happening to her when
she saw his muscles. But she knew that wasn't the case. That
was oversimplifying. She was distracted, and that was un-
forgivable. Because the moment you became distracted, you
revealed your weaknesses. She had done it in the past, and
she refused to do it now. Something about him had drawn
her in, made her lose her sense of time and space, and she
could not allow that to happen again.

"As do I. When would you propose we make this official?"

"Tonight. We had reservations at a private dining room
at a restaurant on the Thames. It was very romantic. We
had a lovely time."

"You really have thought of everything," he said.

"I have. Rest assured that several people saw us ar-
rive, and several people saw us leave looking very happy.
We came and went by way of the back entrance, so it was
only restaurant staff who saw us. Do we have an accord?"

He only looked at her for a moment. Then he nodded his
head once, his expression unchanging. "We have a deal.
Your family company is yours once we terminate the engagement, provided you help me establish my charity."

"Excellent," she said, trying not to betray the utter relief that had washed over her.

"So, what would you have done about your little ruse
had I refused you?"

She laughed, ignoring the twist of nerves in her stomach. She had done it. She had got his yes. Got him to agree, and now she could leave. She could see the light at the end of a tunnel that was more than a decade long. She could have sagged with relief. Melted straight into a puddle of Victoria on the floor.

But up front, she stood firm. "Oh, you were never going to refuse. I knew that. And there were safeguards in place just in case, because I'm tidy like that. But they weren't needed because you were never going to refuse."

His expression hardened and so did his voice. "No," he said, "I don't suppose I was."

"And with that, I bid you good evening. We will be in touch tomorrow to discuss a ring. I'm very classic. I quite like a white diamond."

"And I'm old-fashioned, as well," he said. "I would like very much for my fiancée to be surprised by the choice of ring. Failing that, I shall choose the diamond that is most convenient to me."

She gritted her teeth, annoyance spiking through her. Clearly, he was going to fight her every step of the way. "Do as you see fit." She nodded once and started to walk out of the room, holding her breath as she moved past him, trying to avoid breathing in the fragrance of soap, skin and a scent that she disturbingly suspected was unique to him. But she kept her posture straight, kept herself from acknowledging the fact that she was affected by him. And with that, she strode out the way that she came in.

Victoria Calder intensely disliked places like this, but she did love a victory. And this one was so close she could taste it.

CHAPTER THREE

BY ONE O'CLOCK Dmitri Markin had already had a full day. He had sent his personal assistant after a ring. A yellow diamond in a platinum setting, because he wanted to see what Victoria's reaction would be to his defiance of her order.

He did not take orders, and she would discover that quickly. He also didn't take well to her coming in and attempting to manipulate him, to take full rein of the situation. So he was taking control now.

He had also alerted the media. He'd told them that the two of them had been involved in a covert relationship for the past couple of months, and that last night it had resulted in an engagement. While they were on a dinner date. Which matched up with witnesses' accounts of last night's sighting.

Victoria Calder would realize very quickly that this was his show now. And he would conduct it as he saw fit.

Now all that was left was to speak to his darling fiancée, who was currently five minutes late. He did not take kindly to people running late. Of course, it might've been helpful for him to inform her that she was supposed to meet him with a bit more time for her to actually make the commute to his end of London. She had been somewhere quite a bit away, and traffic would be fairly awful at this time of day, as it was awful at any time of day.

He could very well imagine that *she* hated to be late, and he had all but guaranteed that she would be. The enjoyment he felt at the thought of *her* annoyance did somewhat temper his irritation.

And his irritation vanished completely when she burst through the door of his office, with his assistant on her heels, her blond hair escaping from its neat bun, her cheeks pink.

"So sorry to keep you waiting." Her tone said that she was anything but sorry; in fact it did not denote apology of any kind. In fact, she sounded quite venomous. He found that quite enjoyable.

She had already backed him into a corner, her logic and facts more persuasive than a cattle prod. And here he was again, faced with a fait accompli. Faced with giving away the very last piece of his twisted soul.

He nearly laughed. Perhaps that *would* have been an issue if he'd had a piece of his soul left. Sadly, he was almost certain he didn't. Not even a twisted one.

"I am a very busy man, and I do not like to be kept waiting." He looked behind Victoria's shoulder at his very put-out-looking assistant. "Of course that does not include you, darling."

He could see Victoria's muscles visibly tighten at the endearment, but his assistant's face relaxed. Undoubtedly Louise had been afraid an intruder had got past her.

"Very giving of you, dearest," Victoria sniffed. She crossed the room, and sat in the chair that was positioned in front of his desk.

"That will be all, Louise." His assistant nodded, the relieved expression still on her face as she closed the door. "Nice of you to finally join me."

"Yes, well, I was at a luncheon. I had to leave, quite abruptly. It was very rude. And I am never rude."

"Are you not?"

"Not in public."

"What else don't you do in public?"

She blinked. "A great many things," she said crisply.

"There isn't much I won't do in private. Or in public."
He said it to get a rise out of her, but as the words escaped
his lips, and as the color deepened in her cheeks, he could
not help but experience a rush of heat through his own
veins. Because it made him think of all the things that a
man could do in public, or private, with a woman like Victoria. Truly, there was very little he would not do with her
in either setting. Especially with her.

Then he reminded himself that there was much easier
game to be had. He was working with her, using her to his
advantage, and that meant sex was most definitely out of
the question. Of course, given the fact that they were to
be playing at being a couple, and that introducing anyone
else into their charade would be something of a liability, it
was very likely there would be no sex for the foreseeable
future. The thought made him frown. Deeply.

Victoria frowned in return. "Why do you look so
grumpy? I was only five minutes late."

"I was only pondering the specifics of our arrangement," he said.

That word made her brighten. She seemed to relish this
entire process and he hadn't decided yet if he trusted her.
"Well, talking of specifics, I have drawn up some legal
documents for us to go over."

"That quickly?"

She waved a hand. "Oh, I had these drawn up weeks
ago, when I was first formulating the idea. I know better
than to leave these things until the last minute. The last
thing you want to do a rush job on is legal documents. I
didn't want any reference to our engagement being false

in them, but also I need to guarantee that you will in fact hand over the ownership of my father's company upon the end of our little alliance."

"And what makes you think I'll sign this?"

She shrugged. "Because if you don't, I walk."

"I see." He leaned back in his chair, then pushed against the surface of the desk and stood. "And where is *my* guarantee?"

"If I break off the engagement, then I don't get the company. However, if you break it off, I do. So, if at any point I abandon you, my side of the agreement is void. This is sort of the pre-prenuptial agreement."

"Is that something people do nowadays?"

"Actually, it is."

She reached down and took a folio off the ground, pulling a thick stack of documents out of it. "It outlines several things, including what will become of the ring should we break up—it returns to you—and the fact that I'm not entitled to the company should I break things off with you. It also clearly states that upon our marriage the company reverts to me, but if we divorce and it's my fault, ownership reverts to you. We need all of this seamless. It has to look legitimate even when it's over."

"You certainly don't leave things to chance." He examined her fine features, high cheekbones, the delicate rose color in her cheeks, the faint blush of her lips. She was very pale, her blond hair silvery. To some, he imagined she would appear very fragile, but then, that was what made her interesting. The fact that beneath the soft facade she was steel and ice.

She might appear to be an English rose, but she would not be half so easily crushed.

"Only fools leave these things to chance. Even the best gamblers are calculating odds, not taking wild stabs in the dark." She placed the stack of papers on his desk and pushed them toward his side. He bent to pick them up, slowly leafing through the pages.

"Calculation is important," he said, as he continued to scan the papers. "But you should never underestimate the importance of being able to follow your gut. When you're in a fight there often isn't time to play it out like chess, even if it would be ideal. Sometimes you just have to trust that if you need to feint right, your body will feint right."

"A nice theory. But that has nothing to do with legalities. What do you think?" She looked at him with her sharp blue eyes, her hands folded neatly in her lap.

"Everything looks good." He sat back down behind his desk and opened the top drawer, taking out the ring he had stashed in there earlier. The velvet box made a muted sound as he pressed it slowly onto the wooden surface.

She looked down at the box, then back up at him. "Is that what I think it is?"

"That depends on what you think it is. Perhaps you should open it."

She shot him a look that could only be described as annoyed and reached out, taking the box in her hands. She cracked open the lid and for nearly a full second her expression was blank. Tellingly so. It was very difficult to describe the shift that took place between the look on Victoria's face when she was genuinely at a loss, and the look that appeared when she was trying to make others believe that she was blasé. A subtle softening in her eyes, an added tension around her mouth. It was barely noticeable, but it was there.

By the time she looked up at him she was in full control again. "I told you I don't care for colored diamonds."

"But it suits you. I made an executive decision."

She arched a brow. "It suits me? Or was it just the most convenient diamond?"

A smile curved his lips. "Does it really matter? I've made the decision. This is your ring."

"So that's how this is going to be?"

"Let me make one thing perfectly clear, Ms. Calder. You might have come to me, but the moment I agreed it became *my* game. I do like a challenge, but I also like to win."

She smiled brightly, so brightly that he knew it was false. "That may be a problem, because I like to win, too." She tilted her head to the side, her expression taking on a mock thoughtfulness. "I did a bit of research on your mentor. He was from New Orleans. Is that correct?"

"Yes," he said.

Her expression shifted slightly yet again, and this time the smile seemed more genuine. "Good. That's an excellent venue for charity. And a location people enjoy traveling to. Also, it will appeal to the local moneyed class." He could see her mentally tallying everything up, valuing it.

"You are terrifying. Has anyone ever told you that before?"

"Oh yes." She waved her hand dismissively. "I've been told that on many occasions. But I don't like to be idle, and I don't see the point wasting time—do you?"

"I told you I wanted this rolled out as quickly as possible. Obviously I don't see the point in wasting time. In fact, on that note I have already been in touch with the press to let them know that you and I have decided to marry."

Her pale brows shot upward. "Well, excellent."

"You seem surprised by my efficiency."

"I'm accustomed to being the most efficient half of any partnership. As I'm sure you can well imagine."

"Oh, I can well imagine." He smiled. "But this is the first time you have ever worked with me."

"A mistake, I think. We might make a fairly deadly duo."

"Oh, I am counting on it."

Victoria snapped her folio shut and stood, hands held in front of her, every inch the efficient businesswoman she always seemed. Though, he imagined she wasn't truly a businesswoman. Her reputation was largely as a socialite, and yet she did not appear to be as insubstantial as one tended to assume socialites were. She had all of the strength and steel of someone who was accustomed to doing battle in the boardroom. He knew that she had her own money, mainly from making savvy investments and turning an already-healthy trust fund into a bank account she would be hard-pressed to drain over the course of her lifetime.

He imagined many people underestimated her as a result of her appearance, her petite frame, the fact that she could be easily written off as a lady who lunched and nothing more. He also imagined that some of her strength came from the fact that people underestimated her. Victoria Calder had more dedication, brilliance and determination than half of the CEOs he knew.

"I'll be in touch about the New Orleans charity event. Would you like to set a budget?"

"This is coming out of my pocket, is it?"

She waved a hand, a gesture he was becoming used to. "Of course it is. I'm doing you a service. Naturally you will be paying for it. I will see what I can manage to get donated, of course, but I need to establish a venue, and there will need to be food."

"Louise will send you something." He looked down at his computer for a moment, then back up at her. "I would prefer not to be bothered by the arrangements. I figure our agreement should have as many perks for me as possible.

And somehow I get the impression that planning an event is a perk to you."

"It most certainly is. Especially in New Orleans. In the meantime I will be in touch with the media about the event, and I will let them know how deliriously happy I am to be wearing your ring." She picked the ring box up from the desk. "Even though yellow is not my color."

"I disagree, I think yellow could be your color. You just seem to insist on wearing black." He examined the black pencil skirt and fitted black top she was wearing today. He couldn't deny that she looked striking in black, but still.

"You, too," she said, indicating his suit.

"Touché. We will be in touch." She turned to go. "And Ms. Calder…" She turned back to face him. "You had better make sure to put the ring on. The press will be expecting it."

The right corner of her lips tugged downward, and she reconfigured the things she was holding, opening the ring box and taking the jewel out. Then she slipped it, rather unceremoniously, onto the fourth finger of her left hand. "There—" she wiggled her fingers "—are you satisfied?"

No, dammit, he wasn't. She was too cold by half, too in control. He didn't like it. And before he could question why, he had stood and rounded the desk.

"Not just yet." He closed the distance between them, watching as her blue eyes widened with each step he took nearer to her. "You do not look like a woman who has just had an encounter with her fiancé."

"What do I look like?" she asked, tilting her head to the side, her expression still far too composed. All of the color in her cheeks was courtesy of her makeup.

"A woman who has just been in a business meeting. And I find that unacceptable."

Her hair was already slightly messy from her trek across

the city, but he still felt it wasn't enough. He reached out, pressing his fingers to her temples and sliding his hand backward, fingertips sinking deeply into the softness of her hair. She froze beneath his touch, her eyes widening, her mouth rounding into a perfect O.

He shifted his hold, tugging at the pins that held her bun in place, letting the shimmering locks fall free around her shoulders. He raised his other hand, forking it deeply in her hair, ruffling it slightly as he might have done during a passionate kiss.

For the first time, he thought he might have actually succeeded in shocking her. Oh, certainly he'd had moments of surprising her, such as when he'd taken her up to his apartment in the gym and talked fake engagement logistics in a towel. But he didn't think he had truly shocked her until this moment.

He was only guessing, of course, because of the way that she held herself so still, because of the way that she looked at him, blue eyes wide and lacking in the kind of sharpness they usually held.

There was something soft there now, something blurry.

His stomach tightened, lust grabbing him by the throat and shaking hard. He was on edge with her, a touch bringing him much closer to losing hold on his control than he would like to admit.

There was no denying that he found her very attractive. No denying that she *was* very attractive. And he wanted to know what it would be like to undo all those buttons on her blouse, to push that tightly fitted skirt up around her hips, tease her until she cried out, and then sink into her softness.

He wouldn't do any of those things. She had him in a difficult position, and he would not increase the power she had by giving into this unwanted attraction.

She gasped, as though she had read his mind, as though she had seen into his filthy fantasies. But, though he wouldn't act on them, he was fine with her being aware. Let her know. Let her understand. Let her feel the control slip from her grasp as she realized that he was the one with the upper hand.

That, while he felt the attraction, if he chose to act on it, she would be powerless to resist. That he could have her, begging, naked, if he wanted.

The color heightened in her cheeks, as though he really *had* kissed her. As though he had spoken the words that were running on a loop through his mind out loud.

"That's better." He released his hold on her and took a step backward, much more affected than he should be. Than he cared to be. He had been doing this to exercise control yet again, and yet again, she had tested it. "Now you look much more like a woman who has just been with her fiancé."

"I think the ring would've done it," she said, the crystal edge her voice normally held dulled, replaced by something much more husky. Something thicker, richer. And he knew that would be the voice she would use in bed. Soft like velvet and just as luxurious.

Desire slugged him sharply in the gut and he turned away from her. "That you think the ring would've been enough makes me wonder what you know about relationships, Ms. Calder. Perhaps that is why the engagement to your prince didn't work out?"

It was an unkind thing to say, but he didn't really care. He had never much minded whether or not people saw him as kind. In fact, he generally preferred for people to see him as the grumpy bastard he was.

Which was part of his problem now. He'd taken no pains with his reputation at all. His life had opened up wide when he'd retired from fighting, when he'd earned his money and he'd taken the chance to live it as he saw fit. To live without limits.

Too bad the public didn't appreciate his expression of freedom to the same degree that he did.

"Fortunately for you, Mr. Markin, I do not need to understand personal relationships. I only need to understand how to improve one's image in the media. I only need to understand how to put on a gala and get a charity running, and on that score I am an expert. I'll let you worry about the rest. You seem to be doing an adequate job. I bid you good day."

And when he turned back around she was gone, and he had the inescapable feeling that she had won a round yet again.

Victoria spent the next two weeks fielding congratulatory phone calls from friends and family and putting together plans for the launch of the Colvin Davis Foundation. A venue in New Orleans had been selected, local restaurants were providing food as a donation, she had managed to find a minor celebrity to act as master of ceremonies and she was just generally feeling really good about the decisions she'd been making lately.

Now that all of her overseas responsibilities had been arranged, she was doing one of her favorite things in the world. She was packing for a trip.

She'd never been to New Orleans before so she'd spent the morning researching what she might need to bring, then finding the corresponding items in her closet, making lists of what she didn't have, and planning on when she could buy them.

She and Dmitri would be leaving in just two days. She managed to avoid him in the weeks since they'd made their engagement official. The media was chomping at the bit for a picture of the two of them, but in her mind that was so much the better. Better to leave them wanting than give them too much.

They would make their official debut as a couple at the fantastic and glittering affair she had planned. There, Dmitri would read his mission statement for the charity and cash would flow into the coffers like water flowing forth from a burst dam. She could see it all clearly in her head. More importantly, she could see very clearly the moment when she told her father that she had reclaimed their family business.

The Calder family hadn't been ruined by the loss of London Diva—no, they were far too successful, with many diverse investments.

But money hadn't been the issue. Not really. It was her father's pride.

A man of no significant background, he'd clawed his way into the elite social circles, earning his fortune through hard work. London Diva had been his flagship company, the means by which he'd changed his whole life. And she had lost it.

But of course he had allowed the world to believe that it had been a foolish mistake of his that had cost him the boutique. He had allowed all of those upper-crust snobs to believe they'd been proven right, so that she wouldn't suffer. He had done that to protect her when she had not deserved protection. Even in his anger he had done that for her.

And he had suffered. Invitations to events had all but disappeared, many investors had jumped ship, good friends had proven false. The reputation, the respect her father had worked so hard to achieve, wiped out by one foolish act on her part.

She'd been an idiot with stars in her eyes, feeding vital company information to a man who had so clearly never loved her that just thinking about it now made her cringe.

Yes, the wisdom that came with being a twenty-eight-year-old woman meant that she knew now just how disinterested Nathan had really been. The man had barely kissed her. At the time it seemed romantic. That he was somehow honoring her by refraining from taking her to bed.

The years, and that experience, had made her so much more cynical. She saw it now for what it was. Dear Lord, when a man was trying to take advantage of you and he *didn't* add sex to that, he was so uninterested there was almost no scale by which to measure it.

And when she remembered her ultimate humiliation... No. She *wouldn't* remember it.

She was organizing. She was in her happy place. She pulled out a few of her favorite outfits and walked out of the closet and into her bedroom, laying each carefully hung and wrapped ensemble on the bed. She stood there for a moment regarding them when her phone started buzzing from its position on the comforter.

She saw her father's name and her heart did a shimmy up to her throat. She hadn't spoken to him since she'd made the engagement with Dmitri official. Mainly, she spoke to her father when she went home for dinner with him once a month. Being with him was difficult. Ever since her mistake it had been.

But then, it was sort of difficult to sit down to a meal with someone you'd betrayed so badly, whether or not you'd done it on purpose.

She took a breath to try to dispel the tension in her chest and picked up the phone. "Hello, Dad."

"Hello, Victoria. What is this I see about your engagement?"

He was not one for preamble, her father. "Oh, yes. That. I was going to ring you about that."

She'd intended to ring him about it a couple of weeks ago. She'd intended to ring him about it last week, too. She also intended to ring him about it last night. But every time she had started to dial his number she'd got cold feet. After the way the Stavros thing had blown up she hadn't been feeling very keen. Because she knew that this time her father would be suspicious of it working out, and in the end of course he would be right, because she didn't intend to marry Dmitri. But it wouldn't *matter* in the end because she would have returned what she had lost. Even so, it was a conversation she had been delaying purposefully.

"I confess I did not expect to read about my only child's engagement in the newspaper."

"Yes, well. That is unfortunate. I was quite surprised when Dmitri asked, and given his position the press is all over it of course."

Her father continued on without pausing. "He owns London Diva."

"Yes—" bugger, she had been caught out "—he does. I am aware of that."

"What is it you are doing, Victoria?"

"Getting married." She looked down at her manicured hands. "I am of marriageable age. Past, really. It's about time, honestly. But yes, I was feeling hesitant about calling you because of circumstances being what they are. Dmitri's ownership of what was formerly our family business, and of course my aborted arrangement with Stavros."

"You are in love with him?" It wasn't concern she heard in her father's voice, rather, a cold curiosity.

"Honestly, Dad, I'm much more concerned with practicalities than I am with love. But I am very fond of him."

Her father chuckled. "Neatly done, Victoria. If you had

said that you are madly in love with him I would have known you were lying."

Her father's words disconcerted her somewhat. She had gone out of her way to change. To learn from her mistakes. To think with her head, rather than letting her heart lead. Even so, it did hurt a little bit to hear someone else's assessment of her and her character.

But then, considering she had enlisted the services of a matchmaker to help her find a suitable and dispassionate marriage, she supposed she couldn't blame her father. No, the blame rested squarely with herself. The thing was, she really didn't care much about love, unless she was thinking in terms of avoiding it.

"Right. Well. Not lying. Are you concerned for my well-being…or…?"

"You have a tendency to land yourself on the wrong side of men. Are you sure I won't have another scandal to clean up in the next few months?"

Shame, anger, sadness, threatened to choke her. "Well, I don't plan on it."

"Then what are you planning? What are your goals concerning London Diva?"

Her throat constricted, drying. This was her moment. Much earlier than she had expected to have it. She hadn't intended to say anything until she was able to present him with a document stating legal ownership. But of course he would know that Dmitri was the one who now held ownership, and of course he would be suspicious of the link. She simply wasn't capable of playing stupid.

"My plans are to return London Diva to its rightful place."

There was a brief pause. "We'll see." No vote of confidence. No request she rethink an engagement purely for the sake of the family business. Nothing more. He simply rang off.

His response wasn't surprising. She should expect his indifference and lack of confidence at this point. But it still hurt. Every time.

"I'm going to fix it," she said, the silence of her bedroom only slightly less responsive than her father.

The phone rang again while still in her hand, and she pressed the green icon. "Hello?"

"Hello, darling."

It was Dmitri, the way his accent curled around the endearment making it sound exotic, catching her off guard. Well, obviously she was caught off guard, or she would never apply a word like *exotic* to a silly endearment. Particularly not one designed to make her angry.

"Did you need something?"

"I was wondering how the plans were coming along."

"Just fine. I was getting ready to book tickets. I'm assuming that you're springing for first class," she said, just to needle him. Because her interaction with her father had made her feel low and for some reason pushing against Dmitri brought her a rush of adrenaline that made her feel invigorated.

He chuckled and she held the phone away from her ear. A perk of not being near him in person. She did not have to listen to that unsettling sound. "I was thinking I might do you one better. We're going on my private jet."

"Fantastic. Then I don't have to limit how many pairs of shoes I bring."

"Ah, *milaya moya*, I promise to buy you shoes once we get there."

"Yes, but will you let me choose them? You don't seem to think I should be allowed to choose my own things."

"That depends. I have always been a fan of the kinds

of shoes that make a woman look like she's begging to be bent over a piece of furniture and pleasured until she can't speak."

Victoria couldn't speak *now*. But it had nothing to do with pleasure. Her cheeks were on fire. Her heart pounding so hard she felt dizzy. She swallowed, somehow finding words again. "And what kinds of shoes are those?"

"Stilettos, of course."

She sighed. "Yes, predictable."

"Possibly a little bit. But I guarantee you what happens after the shoes are on is less predictable."

She found herself searching for words again. "I'm packing. Shoes. But what kinds of shoes are irrelevant."

"Glad to hear it. I will see you in a couple of days."

He hung up, and it did nothing to dissipate heat in her face or her body. His unpredictability was something of a liability. And the fact that he had the power to affect her was irritating.

No matter, she was packing now. She was good at packing. And then they were going to New Orleans, and she was going to be in her element orchestrating the event. And she would be in control then. Because this was what she did.

Sure, she had some failures in her life, but not in this arena.

And now that her father knew about the agreement, she would be extra certain that she made it work.

She had to. There was no other option.

CHAPTER FOUR

IT WAS A shock to go from the carefully cultivated comfort of Dmitri's private plane out into the thick afternoon air of New Orleans.

Victoria breathed a sigh of relief as they transferred from the tarmac to the black car that was waiting for them.

The flight over had been uneventful. Victoria had spent the majority of it in the private bedroom trying to get herself on the proper time schedule, even though she knew it would be somewhat futile. Jet lag was very often wicked no matter what tricks she tried to employ en route. But whether or not it helped with her sleep pattern it had helped her avoid Dmitri. That made it worth it.

Yes, she knew that she had to find some more companionable feelings for him, but she wasn't about to do it when she was trapped thirty thousand feet above the ground in a small metal tube with the man. No, thank you. Much better to deal with him when her feet were on solid ground and she was feeling more in control of the situation.

And she would, once they managed to get to their Royal Street accommodations in the French Quarter. It was amazing what money could accomplish, and in this case it meant exclusive use of the boutique hotel for both their event and for the guests making a commute to the event. Dmitri had a lot of money, and that meant there was no end to what she could accomplish. At least seemingly. She also had plans coming together for an event in New York next week with a venue that was nearly impossible to get an entire year in advance, forget less than a month. Following that would be the final launch party in London, which would see the opening of Dmitri's charity as a rousing success, and the closing of their engagement as a rousing one, too. All in closer to a month and a half, rather than three months as she'd originally quoted.

All she had to do was manage the slight tension she felt whenever she was in close proximity with him. And that should be simple.

A little bit of insanity when he ran his hands through her hair in his office was understandable. She had not been inoculated to his magnetism yet. And really, now she thought about it, assuming that you were the one exception to a specific danger was foolishness. And she had to confess, even if only to herself, that she had been foolish going into her dealings with Dmitri.

Because she had spent so many years inured to male charms, she'd assumed it would transfer to him.

Problematically, it had not.

But she wouldn't waste time beating herself up about it. Better women than her had fallen to the likes of him, so there was nothing for it but to simply accept that she found him attractive and move on from it. Finding someone attractive did not mean you had to act on it.

Of course, Stavros had come with a reputation of his own. While not a playboy per se, he was a prince, and a nice-looking one at that, meaning he was custom designed to be irresistible. He'd had his share of lovers, and the other women who had been vying for his affections at the time had been positively giddy over him, while Victoria had remained mainly immune.

She could still remember feeling the most intense sense

of relief the first time he'd nearly kissed her. Not because he'd been about to kiss her, but because in the end, for whatever reason, he had decided not to.

She'd been baiting him, trying to get him to make that all-important lip-to-lip contact, but he hadn't. Later, it had become clear that it was because he had fallen for their matchmaker, Jessica Carter, but at the time she hadn't understood why. Only that she had been extremely happy not to have to deal with a physical relationship just yet.

She simply hadn't been in a space to be dealing with it. She had subsumed all of her sexual feelings after that unfortunate incident with Nathan. Because it had been easier. Because it made things much simpler. It was much easier to keep her eyes on the prize, to keep moving toward the goal of redemption when she wasn't distracted by nonessentials.

Unfortunately, Dmitri was part and parcel of essentials. And whatever had insulated her against Stavros's charms was not working here. She took a deep breath. Oh well, she had acknowledged it. Acknowledging it was the first step to ignoring it, or something like that.

Victoria reached around behind her head and coiled her hair around her wrist, lifting it up off her neck. Her skin was already sticky. "Is there some way we can turn the air-conditioning up?" she asked, keeping her eyes on this view outside. So far the expressway was typical—modern buildings and palm trees whizzing past. There was a creek running alongside the road, and children with small nets trying to catch something in the murky waters.

"I believe it's up as high as it goes."

"It's like a very wet oven," she said, knowing she sounded a bit whiny and a lot snobby. But this was a heat quite unlike anything she'd ever felt before. It wasn't simply the temperature, but the air quality.

"It is that. I take it you've never been here before?"

"No, I haven't been. Have you?"

"I was here once before with Colvin." He kept his eyes fixed on the view outside the window. "This was back when I was still fighting. We came to help hurricane relief. Things were very different then."

"I imagine so."

"I always admired the lengths he went to in order to help others. The lengths he went to in order to help me, and anyone else he felt needed it. Certainly his interest in me wasn't entirely altruistic, as I did end up making him quite a lot of money. But he had no way of knowing that for sure. He had an instinct, he had his gut, but there were no guarantees that sinking hours of free training into an angry street urchin were going to amount to anything."

"How did he end up in London? How did *you* end up in London?"

"I ended up in London by way of Colvin. He went for the usual reason. A woman. Though it didn't work out, because by the time I was on the scene she was not."

"Where did you meet him?"

"Russia."

"Where in Russia?" He simply stared at her, his dark eyes impassive, his chiseled jaw set. He was far too handsome for his own good. For her own good. Really, it was gratuitous. "You realize Russia's a very big country."

"I do." He smiled, somewhat ruefully. "Moscow. I was fighting in bars at the time. Cage matches. Very unsophisticated, very few rules. Lots of blood."

"Oh."

"Yes. I spoke little English, beyond a few foul swearwords. And Colvin spoke no Russian. But he knew potential when he saw it, and he offered me some very good vodka when I desperately needed some, so we sat down to try to have a chat. He was there talent scouting, looking for actual trained fighters. And he wandered into a bar the night that I fought a particularly crushing victory. He told me I had potential, which seemed laughable when I had just left a man stone-cold unconscious in the middle of the cage. In my mind, I was unstoppable. But he told me he would bring me back to London and teach me how to fight for real so that we could both make a whole lot more money."

"And you just went with him? Just like that?"

He lifted his shoulder. "What did I have to fear?"

"I don't know. Going off with a stranger seems rather dangerous."

"Perhaps to you. But I had just demonstrated to the man that I could effectively disable someone with one well-placed hit. I was angry, I didn't fear pain and I had nothing to lose. I was very close to being an animal. I saw no reason not to jump at the chance to escape from Russia, to escape from the hell that I was living in. A chance to fight for more than pocket change and a bed for the night? It was another choice. After years of feeling as though I had none. I was intrigued."

"I can imagine." Although it was very difficult.

Victoria's life had always been very shiny. Very ornate. She lived with the weight of expectation, yes, and it had been far from perfect. Just as she had been. But it was nothing like what Dmitri described. Cage fighting in bars. There was something about the way he said it that was very bleak. Well, she imagined that it was a reality that could sound nothing but bleak. Especially by comparison to her own well-appointed upbringing.

"The first place we went to in London was the gym that you met me in." The gym that had, to Victoria, seemed very low scale.

"It was a palace to me," he said, as though he had just

read her mind. "After the stench in those bars, after the mildew and dampness of the rooms in the cellars and above the places where we fought, where we would sleep with nothing more than a cot and a thin blanket, the accommodations that Colvin offered were nothing short of luxurious. I thought no matter whether or not he made us rich, whether or not he made me famous, I could do no worse than where I already was."

"It must've been…" Victoria searched for the proper words and found she didn't have any. She had no experience in such things, no experience of life under those circumstances. She couldn't imagine viewing the hovel of the gym back in London as though it were a mansion. But Dmitri had. And the realization twisted something inside of her, made her stomach feel tight and strange. Made it feel as if she could scarcely breathe.

"In the beginning it was very frustrating. I expected to be fighting. I expected to be doing more of what I was already doing. But from the first moment I arrived in London, he kept me inactive. At least, to my view. He had me doing training exercises. Basic forms and martial arts. All this stuff that seemed very much like a waste of my time. I used to ask him if he was some kind of ninja master." He laughed at his own memory. "I didn't know very much English when I came to him, but I learned insults very quickly got the point across in any language."

"He trained you in martial arts first?"

"I already had the brute strength down. Already had that cage fighting sensibility. But I lacked in form and technique. And what I lacked in most of all was control. When he introduced me to martial arts I learned that there were better ways. That anger makes an opponent weak. That a lack of form betrays your next move. That by watching those who had inferior technique to myself I could guess where they were going to go next. That's the chess game."

"You told me chess wasn't enough," she said, thinking back to the conversation they'd had in his office. Of course, thinking of that made her think of the moment when he touched her hair. More than touched her hair…caressed it. Ran his fingers deep through it.

She tried to ignore the rising tension in her body.

"It isn't. That's why Colvin reminded me to keep with me what I already had. My gut. Intuition. Training combined with raw talent made me an unstoppable fighter in the ring. And from there I got my sponsorships."

"How does a boy from the streets of Moscow go from fighting in bars to owning one of the largest conglomerates of retail shops in the world?"

"From my sponsorships came modeling opportunities. Which, as you can guess, weren't really my thing. But that gave me the opportunity to work very closely with the owner of an athletic wear company, Sport Limited. I gave him some suggestions on how to tweak some of the gear we were using. I ended up with my own line. He told me I had a good head on my shoulders, that I had a good mind for business. So, I took some of the money I had been earning in my fights and started taking classes. When Hugh was ready to sell Sport Limited, I had the money and the know-how to take it over. From there, I started buying out more places. Failing retail lines that I felt that I could revamp."

"You ended up with London Diva," she said, an empty statement of fact that served very little purpose. Just a reminder for her. Of why she was here. Of the real point of his story, of all of this.

"Yes. For a while I bought up everything I possibly could. And it turned out I had an eye for where to place certain stores, and for what the next high-demand items might be. I have done well. My world expanded after Colvin took me in, after he taught me and trained me. I began to think about more than just where my next meal might come from, or where I might sleep that night. It changed everything for me. It opened up a whole new world of possibilities.

"I want to do that for these children who might come into my gym. Into these gyms that will hopefully be established by the foundation. I want to provide not only training, but the kind of emotional support that I received. It changed who I was. I was fueled by anger when I lived in Russia. The path I was on was narrow. And it had one end. But when I went to England? That was when I saw all the different directions that path could turn. And it all started with a simple bit of training that I resented so much at first."

"It's an amazing story." Victoria swallowed hard. "One I feel people cannot help but be moved by. You should tell it when you give your speech at the charity gala this week."

"You want me to speak?"

"Well, it is your charity."

"Didn't you get a celebrity emcee?"

She lifted a shoulder. "I did, but I think you'll find it will be much more powerful for you to share your personal story. Celebrities are only marginally impressed by other celebrities."

He titled his head to the side, one dark brow lifting. "You may not realize this, but some people find me offputting."

She raised her brows and gave him her best surprised look. "Indeed. I guessed something like that."

"I thought you might have. Though, most women are much more fond of me than you seem to be."

Victoria's cheeks heated "Well, most women are after something different than I am. Which is the source of many of your issues with the press. Seeing as you are a... let me see if I can call up some of the finer terms used to describe you... A manwhore. A home wrecker. A corruptor of innocents."

"I've never corrupted an innocent in my life," he said, his tone casual. "The rest of it is probably true." He shifted in his seat, one long leg bent at the knee, his elbow resting on it, his chin resting on his hand. He looked too large to be contained in such a small space, too feral to be enclosed in something so luxurious. Reflecting on the time since she'd met him, Victoria decided he was a man who never seemed to fit into his surroundings. Not entirely at the gym, and not entirely here, either. There was something more to him, and she couldn't quite put her finger on it.

Something intriguing, which made it dangerous. Because she should not be intrigued by him. Not now, not ever. He was simply a means to an end; he was nothing to get excited about.

She cleared her throat. "Either way, I think you will be well served to share your story. I found it inspiring."

"Did you, Victoria? If so, I'm surprised."

"Why is that?"

"You don't seem the type to be moved by human interest pieces."

Victoria wasn't quite sure how to take that. "I'm not sure what you mean. I have been celebrated for my work in charity."

"I fail to see what charity work has to do with the way things actually make you feel. You seem a woman more motivated by the bottom line than by altruism."

She made an indignant sound. "I love altruism. I'm a huge fan of it. I also like people to be fed. I like them to have shelter. I don't think I like the personality that you seem to be ascribing to me." His words stung a bit. But it wasn't as if she was doing a good job of being honest with him about how much her charity work meant to her. But it was personal, and she didn't like to share personal.

In her experience, sharing personal pieces of herself only led to rejection. It was one thing to risk that for her father, or for the man she'd thought herself in love with. She saw no point risking that with Dmitri.

"Do not be offended. I am merely saying it as I see it. I am not a man given to sentimentality, either. Except in this case. Except where Colvin, and his legacy, are concerned. Because of what he did for me personally I want him remembered, what he did remembered. And more importantly, I want the essence of who he was to keep living."

Well, now she felt slightly guilty for withholding honesty since his response was completely genuine. She cleared her throat. "Good. Channel all of that into a speech about how incredibly your life changed because of your experiences with martial arts and the opportunities the mind-set opened up to you."

The scenery had started to change, the buildings growing older as they went deeper into the city. A track line for trolleys ran through the center of a busy street, lined with large hotels, fast-food restaurants and upscale boutiques, as though everything had sort of crashed into each other and settled like this.

They turned off the main drive, all of the architecture here reminiscent of things more commonly found in Europe than in the United States. But there was something else, too. An open friendliness to go with the stateliness that was unlike any place she had ever been before. Magnolia trees grew on the sidewalks, large white blossoms punctuating the dark green leaves, strands of colored beads trapped in the branches, like Christmas decorations that had been left behind.

The buildings were connected, tall and narrow, made from stone with ornate iron balconies that wrapped around the facades. And every few feet there were signs hanging down from the balconies, advertising rentals that came in two varieties: haunted and non.

"I forgot to ask about ghosts." She was trying to lighten up the topic of conversation now. Trying to move it away from his personal take on her as a human being, which she was almost certain she didn't like it all. "It appears there are ghostly options here. I hope very much I have not put us on the wrong side of those options."

He waved a hand. "It's New Orleans. As far as I know every place has its ghost, and if it doesn't…the owners are lying."

"I don't want any ghosts coming in and spoiling our party."

"How do you know they would spoil it? They may very well enhance it."

"For a man who is so confident in his ability to manage the ghosts of the past, you seem open to the idea of them coming into the present."

"Someone else's ghosts are fine. It's my own that I prefer to keep buried."

That made her laugh. "I'll drink to that. In fact, perhaps we should, later."

"An excellent idea."

The car came to a stop in front of a pink building that wrapped around a street corner. It was three floors high with hanging plants and vines growing over the balconies, doing their part to obscure the windows, and those who might be behind them, from the street below.

"This is it," she said, "I recognize it from the pictures online."

"An excellent venue—I have faith that those who came looking for something uniquely New Orleans will be satisfied."

Victoria certainly hoped so. She had made sure to tell him that there would be no guarantees on her end of the deal. After all, there was no way she could force people to change their opinion of him. But the fact remained that she wanted to do the best job possible. It was important to her, because when she said she would do something, she felt she'd better bloody well do it. The fact was she had enough of letting people down. Yes, it had been only one major mistake, but it had been a *major* mistake. One her own father could scarcely forgive her for.

She had never felt clean after. She wasn't sure she ever would. Wasn't sure if she would ever be able to obliterate the stain from her record. But she had to try, she had to. That was why she was here now. That was why she was doing her damnedest to accomplish this for her father, and suddenly, she felt driven to accomplish this for Dmitri, as well.

He meant nothing to her, not personally. But his story was compelling, his goal was noble.

He spoke about how Colvin had changed his life and that made her want to be a part of this. It made her want to change the lives of the children his program would impact. Because if Dmitri Markin could come from a dirty bar in Moscow, Russia, to be one of the wealthiest men in all of Europe, then truly anything was possible. Even reconciliation with her father.

And she knew she wouldn't be the only one who came away from this week's gala feeling that way.

"I do hope you brought suitable gowns," he said.

"Of course I brought suitable gowns. I have an entire closet full of nothing *but* suitable gowns. It is all but my profession to attend these kinds of events."

"Yes, I do realize that. But you're not attending as Victoria Calder. You are attending as Victoria Calder, lover to Dmitri Markin, and my lovers have standards."

She snorted. "Maybe you have raised your standards since the last time you appeared with a lover."

He laughed and opened the back door to the car, leaving her sitting in the air-conditioned space by herself. She unbuckled and scrambled out her side, stumbling as she placed her foot on the uneven pavement just outside the vehicle. "Good Lord." She righted herself. "Just one second," she said. "What exactly do you think is so funny? I'm very classy."

"In my experience, Victoria, when someone has to tell you they *are* something, they are not it."

She spread her hands. "I exude class."

"Certainly you do." He regarded her closely, looking up and down as though she was a car he was interested in buying and not a human being. "The problem is my lovers tend not to."

"I thought we went over this. The press would expect you to be with a woman who had a little bit of fight in her. Maybe ultimately the press will be expecting for you to end up with a woman who doesn't fit your normal repertoire."

"Perhaps." He rounded to her side of the car and knocked on the front passenger window. The driver rolled it down. Dmitri leaned in. "Have the bags sent up. I need to get Ms. Calder out of the car as I believe the Southern weather has thoroughly rumpled her rather delicate English temperament."

Victoria harrumphed. "My delicate English temperament," she muttered. "You're from Russia. I would've expected you to melt by now."

"I'm not that easy to get rid of." He turned his broad back to her, the sun glinting off the black fabric of his suit jacket. She was roasting just looking at him. He began to walk in toward the hotel entrance and she followed, dodging the dips and dents in the sidewalk. She had read online about the sidewalks in New Orleans being notoriously bad, but she had still worn high heels for travel day, and she was starting to question the sanity of that. Fortunately, she had brought an entire suitcase filled with sensible shoes for when she would be walking outside the hotel. The kinds of shoes that did not ask a man to bend her over anything and do anything to her.

The memory of that interaction made her face burn.

Her face still burned even when they walked into the very ornate lobby. The air was cool inside, but it did nothing to make her feel any less hot and bothered. Though, she imagined that the heat Dmitri made her feel was completely independent of the heat outside. It had to be, because she'd been hot since before they left England.

Acknowledging it is the first step to dealing with it. So deal with it, Victoria.

She had to; she had no other choice. Because the only other option was giving in. And she had already vowed that she would never do that, never again.

Dmitri found himself fascinated by Victoria, and he found that fascination annoying. She was icy, she was prickly—in short, she was a female version of himself. Though, he knew how to be softer with a lover. Victoria seemed capable of being only one way with him. She did not seem capable of playing a part. It should bother him because it put their entire ruse in jeopardy. But it didn't, or rather, it *did*, but only in the sense that it made him determined to figure out a way beneath the hard shell exterior she wore around her like armor.

They had gone their separate ways once they were inside the hotel, Victoria saying she needed a shower to get rid of the film of stickiness she had accumulated over her skin since landing in Louisiana. He had not seen reason to argue, though he had wanted to stay with her, not wanting to give her reprieve, not wanting to give her the chance to rebuild her control. And he could have stayed with her, seeing as they were sharing a multiroom suite in the interest of keeping up appearances, but he had not.

Because he felt as if every time they parted she had her walls back up even more firmly than before they left each other.

Because the fact was, he seemed to be breaching them to a degree. A triumph if ever there was one, though, only depending on how you looked at it.

He should not want to be intrigued by Victoria, not on a personal level. But the fact remained that he was. She was as beautiful as she had been the moment he had first seen her, and as bad an idea as she had been from that moment, too. His body did not seem to care. His body seemed to think that because she was wearing his ring, no matter the terms, she should also be in his bed.

His stomach tightened, blood flowing south, making him hard.

Yes, there was no denying that he was physically intrigued by Victoria.

Though right now she seemed intent on denying him her presence. He had asked her to meet him down in the lobby, where he was currently waiting for her, and she was most definitely late.

He looked around the room, at the marble walls and

floors. Crystal chandeliers hanging from the ceiling. He was used to this kind of ornate architecture. It was everywhere in London. Finely done architecture, intricate stonework. Everything that glittered most definitely gold. And yet, every time he was in a new place, he found himself admiring it all the same. As though it were the first time.

He found that no matter how much he wanted to be, he could not be jaded about this kind of beauty. The same way he could not be jaded about the type of beauty Victoria had.

He had been with many women, most especially since his rise to fame and fortune. And at this point, one beautiful woman should be same as the next. But they weren't. They never were. Soft luxuries in his life he appreciated, every time, without fail.

Victoria all the more. Because she had a particular quality of luxury to her that was almost indefinable. She was the painting in the museum flanked by guards. Cordoned off by thick velvet ropes and signs that warned you it was okay to look but never to touch. She was the next level of luxury. And she was everything he craved, whether he should or not.

The fact remained that when there was art around that could be touched, could be purchased easily, it made no sense to covet the piece that was unattainable.

It made no sense, but it was human nature.

Which was why he desired Victoria, though he should not.

The plane ride over had not even been helped by the fact that she had spent most of it hiding in the bedroom. He had still been intensely aware of her presence. As he had been intensely aware of her in the car. That awareness had caused him to lower his guard. Had caused him to spill forth the kind of honesty he rarely allowed.

His past was not impossible to discover. Even so, he often avoided speaking about it. There were no happy memories back in the mists of time. Nothing he liked to revisit.

With her, the story had seemed easy to tell. He had *wanted* to tell her, and he could not quite understand why. To make her understand? To make her see the gravity of it all? Why he needed things to work out as he did. Yes, that made sense, and he could not be faulted for that. Because this charity felt essential to him, and he did not want her to view it as having any less importance.

He felt her come into the foyer before he saw her, every muscle in his body tensing, his nerves on high alert. And then he saw a fine-boned, pale hand resting on the banister, followed by a slender ankle on the stairs, then her foot in a pair of elegant, flat shoes pressing down on the rich burgundy carpet of the bottom step.

And then finally the rest of her was in sight. Her golden hair cascading around her shoulders, slender curves outlined to perfection by a pair of ankle-length pants that conformed to her curves and a flowing top in a slate gray.

The outfit was demure in every sense of the word, and yet, perhaps for that specific reason it was unspeakably arousing. It revealed not a flash more skin than was strictly necessary, and that false sense of the demure managed to capture his imagination in ways that something more revealing never could.

That made him wonder if perhaps he was a bit more jaded than he had ever given himself credit for. If the endless array of models and flashier women had finally become monotonous. If his array of choice had spoiled him.

Though, until meeting Victoria, he had not been aware of them seeming monotonous. No, in fact he had been very happy with his sex life. And with his choice of sexual partners. It was only since meeting Victoria that he experienced a different desire. As though discovering delicacies he had not known existed before. Delicacies his body had now decided it craved beyond all else.

"So," she said, the pristine crystal tone back firmly in place, as formal as their surroundings. "Are you going to take me for that drink you promised?"

"I had thought we might take a few moments together. If for no other reason than to make sure we are on the same page when it comes to the gala."

"That seems like a good idea."

"And yet, you seem annoyed with me."

She waved her hand, his ring glittering on her fourth finger, catching the light from the chandelier and putting the crystals above their heads to shame. "Not any more than usual. I should have liked to recede into my bed and enjoy a little bit of room service, but I will not be seriously wounded by going out, either."

"Well, I'm glad to hear that. That you would not be seriously wounded, that is." She had a look on her face that he had come to recognize as being very practiced. It was not a natural facial expression—that was for certain. It was one that was pulled tight, schooled into a smoothness that simply didn't ring true. He had seen it break so rarely, the only time in recent memory the moment in his office when he had sifted his fingers through her hair, when he had treated her like a lover and not a business partner.

Well, not so much like a lover as he might've liked.

"Shall we go?"

"Yes, we shall. You'll be pleased to know that I have arranged for us to dine privately on the balcony here in the hotel."

"*Dining* even? A whole meal? I was expecting just one drink."

"That's the thing with me, Ms. Calder, I don't do anything by halves."

And that right there caused a blush of color to blossom in her cheeks. That subtle innuendo caused a disturbance in her otherwise-unruffled appearance.

She felt it, too. This thing between them. It made his blood run hotter. And it made him want to push.

"Is that a promise, Mr. Markin?" Her tone was as cold as ever, but he knew the truth now. It was written over her pale skin, a rose-colored letter signifying her body's interest.

"Oh, yes. It is a promise. For you most especially. Should you ever want to test me, I will be more than happy to rise to the occasion."

He could see that she knew he was baiting her, knew that he was taking the conversation away from neutral territory, that he was moving things into the realm of the sexual, which he had purposed upon first meeting her not to do.

He had never been a capricious man; his lifestyle had never lent itself to that. At least not the lifestyle he had found himself in when he'd been cast onto the streets.

From that moment on, planning had been of the utmost importance, finding a course and staying it.

But right now he was contemplating going off-plan altogether. Considering what it might be like if he were to ignore the chess game and surrender to what felt inevitable. He prized his control above all else—men who came from the depths that he had come from could afford to do nothing else. Because he knew what it was like when he let his emotions wreak havoc in his life. And when you came from a place where you let your anger control you, you held no control. There was nothing but blood, nothing but violence. And after that, nothing but an endless well of anger, a black pit that had no bottom that he had seemed to fall through endlessly, waiting for a crushing end to the fall that had simply never happened.

It had been eternal darkness. It had been hell.

Until Colvin had lifted him out of it and shown him a better way. Sure, it was a painful road. One paved with blood and broken bones, but it was no more than he'd deserved. He couldn't imagine a more fitting exit from his personal hell.

Yes, there were many reasons he had purposed to live a life that was led by something other than emotion. Reasons he had buried his old self, and risen again new, clean, different. A baptism by blood and pain, in the truest sense. He'd had to be born again, to accept what he'd become so he could move on, and so he had been. He had not lied when he'd told Victoria that.

She had forced them together and he resented that. It made it all the more important that he not indulge his desire for her because he'd been manipulated into this and he would not let her lead him around by his male anatomy in addition to everything else.

But, with her so near, golden hair so soft, so tempting and close enough to touch again, to wrap around his finger, he wanted to indulge.

You want to go back to that again? To having no choice? To having your hand forced?

His stomach tightened hard as memory closed in around him.

Overwhelming fear, blinding rage, a gunshot and a scream in the air, leaving his entire life shattered, never to be mended again.

No, he could not pursue this.

Control was everything, and the fact that he had forgotten that even for a moment, the fact that he had been on the verge of justifying giving in to temptation meant that he could not.

"It's just upstairs, Victoria. Shall we go?" he repeated, reminding himself of why they were here, what they were doing.

She treated him to one of her tightly controlled smiles. If anything, he should use Victoria as an example of how he should behave. He should admire the fact that she didn't break, rather than being tempted to shatter her.

"An excellent idea, Mr. Markin. I eagerly look forward to our dinner."

He extended his arm, and she curled her own around it. He tried to ignore the flash of heat that rioted through him.

But this was not settled. Nothing was inevitable. Not even this.

He didn't have to give in.

"As do I."

CHAPTER FIVE

THERE WAS NO one else out on the hotel balcony; there was nothing else save one table set for two, crisp linen laid over the surface. Two chairs were placed opposite each other, a low flickering candle in the center. It was designed to be the perfect romantic dinner. Too bad Victoria wanted no part of romance where Dmitri was concerned, and very much too bad that she had to play as though she did anyway. But they could not afford to break character, not even here, not even for one moment.

Of course that meant sharing a room while they were in New Orleans, but fortunately she had been able to book them in a suite that was large enough they might as well be staying down the hall from each other. He hadn't come up to the room during her shower, and as long as he maintained his distance she would be fine.

This—this dinner set out here in the ever-darkening evening—for whatever reason, felt even more intimate than the shared suite. Perhaps because they were on display, which should make it seem less intimate, but given the nature of their arrangement, it did not.

It was starting to get dark outside, the gas lamps that lined the streets of the quarter flickering on, casting an orange glow on everything beneath him. Where they sat she could hear the noise beginning to pick up on Bourbon Street just around the corner. If they rounded to the

other side of the hotel they would be able to get a view
of the revelers, and Victoria had to admit that part of her
was curious. New Orleans had a reputation for being a
city that stripped you of inhibition, and since Victoria had
been firmly attached to her inhibitions since that great,
final humiliation, she found she was slightly interested in
what the city might look like now. Something like wanting
to observe a foreign culture and gain an understanding.

That was it. It had nothing to do with the man who was
currently crossing the balcony and moving to the roman-
tically laid out table. Nothing to do with the fact she was
intrigued by what it might mean to lose her inhibitions
with Dmitri.

No, she was not considering that.

He held her chair out for her, and she smiled in a fashion that she was certain was exceedingly gracious and
sat down.

Dmitri took his place at the table across from her. "The
meal will be served soon. It's prix fixe, so I hope there is
nothing you are exceptionally unfond of."

"I can't imagine anything served at a place like this
wouldn't be wonderful."

"The city does have a great food reputation."

"And I am very excited to partake of it." She looked
around at the empty balcony. "I would also like that drink."
Something to take the edge off being so near to the man.

As if on cue, hotel waitstaff appeared, one brandishing
a bottle of wine and the other with a plate of appetizers.
The first employee set about pouring the wine while the
second laid the plates in front of them laden with a salad
with softshell crab, and set about explaining the dishes
that they would be eating that evening.

Then they both bowed out quickly, leaving Victoria
alone with Dmitri again.

"You are satisfied with how things for the event are shaping up?" Dmitri asked, lifting his glass of wine to his lips.

Victoria wrapped her hands around her own glass, running her fingers over the smooth, cool surface. "Yes, I'm quite happy. Things are coming together much more smoothly than I could've anticipated. Especially given the time frame. I'm particularly surprised with how things are coming together in New York and London."

"Pleasantly, I hope."

"Very. Not only that, it appears that the press is deciding that you are changing, after all. Your commitment to me solidifying that you are indeed going in a new direction."

"I gather they will be terribly disappointed when our engagement ends."

"No, they won't," she said, lifting her glass. "They will be thrilled because they have something new to report on. Happiness gets stale after a while. They really don't like that."

"For someone whose past has been so alarmingly free of scandal, you seem to know the inner workings of the press quite well."

"Because I pay attention, because I am aware that there are certain things I need to avoid. It has always been my aim and intention to keep my reputation as spotless as possible." Which was true enough, cutting out the period in history where she hadn't thought much of it at all. When she hadn't thought about much of anything beyond herself.

"I imagine having grown up in the spotlight is a different experience to having come into it later."

"Yes, I cultivated in awareness fairly early." She had no illusions that she had escaped the iron fist of the press by mere luck. It was fortunate that her father had had no desire to uncover her, that Nathan, for all his sins, had simply wanted London Diva and not to humiliate her or crow about the methods by which he had won his victory.

Though sometimes she thought that the lack of crowing, the lack of open cruelty...the *pity* he'd looked at her with when she'd bared her body to him...was much worse than disdain.

She shook off the memories, the encroaching shame. None of it mattered now. That part of her didn't matter.

"I confess that when I was thrust into the spotlight I had very little awareness for how the media could impact my life and what I wanted to do with it. In fact, until recently I hadn't given it much thought, because it had never prevented me from achieving an aim. I've never cared what people thought of me, never minded that I was seen in a negative light based on how I had come into my fortune, based on the number of women that I'm seen with. Until now."

"I suppose that has to do with several fundamental differences between the two of us."

"Such as?"

She took a sip of her wine. "Well—" she set the glass back down on the table, smoothing the wrinkles of the cloth down around it "—for a start, I'm from a wealthy background. Second-generation money and all. I'm not exactly self-made."

"And the other difference?"

"I'm a woman. So while your reputation might have always been bad, it was in that way people like men to be bad. It's considered rather rakish and charming when you're male, isn't it?"

"Until you want to run a charity for children. Then you're suddenly a monster of some kind not fit for polite society."

"Oh no, once you get children involved they trump all. Think of the children."

"You are quite cynical, Victoria. For someone who has had a life as charmed as yours."

His words made her chest tighten. She ran her fingertips over her arm, feeling the moisture left behind by the heavy air. "I have had a privileged upbringing, I won't deny that. But I also learned a very valuable lesson early on about human nature. Having my blinders ripped off so effectively made me look at things differently. It made me look at people and their motives differently. I have never been able to take people at face value, not since that happened."

"And now I'm intrigued. What exactly did happen?"

Bugger. She thought about lying to him, and truly, she would be justified. Because it wasn't his business, and it had nothing to do with their agreement. Nothing at all to do with their interaction, or her relationship—if you could call it that—with him. But she'd never been the type who lied well on her feet—she excelled in being blunt and straightforward, and putting people on the back foot with that method. Subterfuge wasn't in her bag of tricks. Sadly.

"When I was sixteen my father introduced me to a friend. A business associate of his. He was incredibly handsome, in his early thirties and I developed a massive crush on him from the first moment I laid eyes on him."

"This is not starting where I imagined it might," he said, and she could see that the muscles in his body had started to tense.

Yes, well, if he thought it was going to be difficult for him to hear, he had no idea how difficult it would be for her to say.

"I don't imagine it is. However, this is where it begins. I developed an instant attraction for him. It was nothing like I'd ever felt before. I had always felt like boys my age were rather silly and it had been easy to ignore them in favor of my studies. This was different." She looked up and met Dmitri's gaze, refusing to look down, refusing to look as ashamed as she felt. "Nathan was different. At least, I thought he was. I think he knew how I felt, too, immediately. I think, perhaps, I was terribly obvious. Either way, he found ways to get in touch with me. Excuses to drop by and discuss business with my father when my father wasn't there. And over the course of that time we were able to talk quite a bit. I fell for him, hard. You can't imagine how hard. I thought he loved me, and I certainly loved him. And when the line of questioning changed to my father's business affairs I didn't think anything of it, because he worked with my father on various projects and seemed to be his friend. And I trusted him. But I let slip some very crucial information about a new fashion line, and Nathan gave the information to a competing company. They stole our ideas out from under us, launched their products first and sent London Diva's stocks into a spiral. From there, Nathan purchased the majority of the shares and ousted my father. Because of me. So you can see, it's my responsibility to get it back. And you can see where I learned to start questioning the motives of others."

She looked back up at Dmitri's face. The expression there could only be described as murderous. He opened his mouth as though he was about to say something when the hotel staff returned with different plates of food. They waited while their entrées were placed in front of them, and she watched Dmitri as he watched the staff leave.

Then he turned back to face her, his dark eyes fierce. "Any man that age who takes advantage of a sixteen-year-old girl is no man."

She huffed. "Oh, you get no argument from me, but the fact remains I was instrumental in the loss of my family business. Nathan acted badly, but I was a fool. It's my responsibility to rectify that mistake. And I am doing so."

"I don't see how it's your responsibility to atone for the sins of others."

"Because I'm the only one who cares to atone for them. You don't see Nathan hanging around groveling, offering to return London Diva to the Calder family."

"Well, in part because he can't. Because I bought it out from underneath him."

Victoria couldn't conceal the smirk that curved the right-hand corner of her mouth upward. "So you did. I knew I liked something about you."

"It does not surprise me that you like the rather more cutthroat part of me."

"It shouldn't. I admire it because I had to change after I made that mistake. I knew I had to fix the way that I saw the world and the way that I acted within it. I had always been a good daughter, and I had never done anything wrong, but it didn't matter because I made a mistake that cost my family greatly. I might as well have been rebellious for all of my life. A couple of piercings and tattoos would've been a lot less costly."

Dmitri stretched his arm out across the table, pushing his white shirtsleeve up past his elbow, revealing the intricate tattoo on his forearm, the leather cuff that bisected it. "The right kind of tattoo is fairly costly."

She looked down at his arm and tried to ignore just how dry her throat had got. But there was something about the web of artistry over his tanned, muscled arm that caused a visceral reaction in her.

Who was she kidding? There was something about him that caused a reaction in her. All of her. And all of him.

So different in many ways from that thwarted love affair from years ago, when she'd thought to give Nathan her body because of an intense emotional longing.

This feeling was no less longing, but it had nothing to do with emotion. And it was just as undesirable.

"Still not as expensive as losing an entire chain of clothing stores, I fear. Then, you should know since you bought an entire chain of clothing stores."

"I have bought several of them," he said, his tone light.

"And I only care about the one."

"And I see why now."

She tilted her head to the side. "Were you not curious about it before?"

He drew his hand back and pushed his shirtsleeve back down. Then he lifted one shoulder in a casual shrug. "A little. But then, I figure we all have our secrets. And since I am not the sort of man who likes to share his, I don't expect other people to, either."

"Except, then you asked me to."

"My patience has its limits," he said, his lips curving upward into what could only be described as a deadly smile.

Something about that smile made her stomach tighten further. Suddenly, the sound of raucous cheering broke through the tension, and Victoria breathed a sigh of relief. She really needed a break from whatever intensity was building between the two of them.

This whole acknowledging that she found him attractive thing was supposed to alleviate the issue. Sadly, it was not.

"I wonder what's going on down there."

"Probably a hen night or bachelorette party of some kind. This is a very popular location for them."

"I've never really understood the appeal of them."

"Of a bachelorette party?"

"Yes. They're…not really the sort of thing I can see enjoying."

"Why is that?" he asked.

"What? You'd like a stag party? Strippers and booze and lots of people standing around leering?"

He chuckled. "No. I like strippers just fine, but a private room is more my style."

She didn't know why, but the idea that he enjoyed strippers disappointed her. It shouldn't, because she shouldn't be surprised and she shouldn't care at all. But she did.

"Well. That's something at least," she said.

"Oh, Victoria, you need to learn to let out a breath," he said, leaning back in his chair, his arm slung indolently over the back, his leg stretched beside the table, rather than being shoved beneath.

"What does that mean? That I'm uptight? If you have a question as to why, I refer you to the personal tête-á-tête we had only moments ago."

"One mistake and you have to change who you are forever?"

"One life-altering mistake that ruined things for my family. That destroyed the relationship I had with my father and lost him the respect of his peers."

"Do you suppose Nathan changed because of you?"

The question hit her in the face like a cold, wet rag. "No," she said, feeling her insides constrict, tightening into a ball. "I don't suppose he did. Well, his life changed on some score since he obviously got a chain he was very invested in acquiring so I changed his…life for the best. Oh, that utter bastard."

"Time does not heal every wound."

"No," she said, her tone fierce. "I'm hoping an engagement arrangement resulting in my getting London Diva back will cure my more serious wounds, though."

"It's a good plan."

The servers returned and whisked their plates away, replacing them with the very famous beignets, topped with a mountain of powdered sugar and served with café au lait.

"Lovely," she said, reaching for the small white mug.

"Before we indulge," he said, the word sounding far more wicked than she would like, "I say we go and see the happy partiers of Bourbon Street."

She was curious. Whether she should be or not.

"All right. When in Rome...observe the Romans I suppose."

"But don't step into the arena?"

"As we are not citizens of Rome, I suppose that might be our fate." She picked up her mug and raised it high. "Those who are about to die salute you." She took a sip, then placed it back onto the table before standing and smoothing down her pants. "Now, let's go gawk at some revelry."

She followed him around the curving balcony to the side of the hotel that provided a view of Bourbon Street, the hub of debauchery in New Orleans. At least, the hub of *open* debauchery. She imagined private debauchery took place any number of locations.

The streets below were packed full of people, holding up traffic at cross streets. They were carrying open glasses of alcohol and weaving back and forth.

Women in lingerie were standing in front of shops beckoning passersby to come in, and group of men lingered in front of a club wearing next to nothing, calling out to people, too. And then she saw them, a group of women in black, waving up to the balconies, and one lone woman in white, a tulle veil covering her hair.

"That would be the hen do," she said.

"I imagine so."

She crept closer to the edge of the balcony, using the bride's bright white ensemble as her focal point. "They are…"

"Very drunk."

"To say the least."

She wondered what it would be like to be down there, soaking in the light from the neon and the gas lanterns, right in the middle of the party instead of hovering so far above it. She was always above it. And that was really how she liked it. But still…she wondered.

She felt Dmitri move in closer to her, felt his heat as he closed the distance between them.

Her breath caught in her throat, the sultry night air thick and somehow sensual now, where before, with the sunlight shining through, it had been a bit overbearing. Now somehow it seemed erotic.

And she had no clue what she was doing applying that description to anything. She was not the sort of woman to think of things in those terms. But then, she wasn't the sort of woman to get dry mouth at the sight of a tattoo and a little bit of forearm muscle. And yet, with Dmitri she seemed to be.

Suddenly, she ached. Ached for all the things she hadn't had. For the normal everyday desires that had been stolen from her when she was sixteen, ripped away from her along with her father's company and her trust. In other people. In herself.

Replaced instead with shame—shame about her feelings, her body, her judgment.

If not for that, she might have been down there, too. Maybe had a group of girlfriends she could relate to, and she could drink with and trust that they would lead her back to the hotel unharmed. She might have had a man waiting to marry her the following weekend. One she might have loved. One who might have even loved her back.

One who would take her to bed and give her pleasure. Hold her all night.

Yes, for some reason the sight of all of that normalcy below made her very acutely aware of just how abnormal she was. Just how separate.

But she wasn't all alone, not as she usually was. Dmitri was here. So close she could feel the heat from his body. And a voice deep inside of her spoke clearly enough and loudly enough that she could understand. She wanted to touch the heat. She didn't want to be alone. She didn't want to be cold. Here where everything was so warm, why shouldn't she be?

As though he had read her thoughts, he placed a hand on her waist, leaning in, his lips brushing the shell of her ear. "And what do you think of the party?"

"I've never been a part of anything like that. I mean, at university I saw parties like that, but I never took part in them."

He moved his thumb up and down, smoothing it over the indent of her waist and leaving a trail of fire in its wake. "You never let yourself play, do you? Are you always so good?"

"The way I see it," she said, her voice, her breathing so obviously labored, "we get a certain amount of mistakes allotted to us in the beginning. If we overplay our hand we might lose everything. I overplayed my hand. My mistake amounted to a whole lot and I've never seen the point in taking a risk since. I feel I was lucky not being disowned entirely after putting my father's livelihood and reputation at risk the way that I did. You know, Nathan was married." The reason he had never touched her, which had become clear later. While Nathan had seen no issue with luring her into an emotional affair, he clearly hadn't seen it as being unfaithful so long as he didn't reciprocate and so long as he didn't touch her.

They had kissed but nothing more. Not for a lack of trying on her part. That last night together, before she'd found out the truth, she'd met him in her room, naked. And he'd…he'd covered her with a blanket. As though she were a child. Not a woman. As though there was nothing remotely arousing or sexual about her.

Sometimes, after she had discovered the truth about him, she'd lain awake at night imagining him going over the game plan with his wife. Imagining him gaining permission to kiss her and touch her over her shirt. To tell her that he loved her, as long as he never entered her body, as long as he never really meant what he said.

She imagined them laughing at how easy a conquest she would be. Imagined him telling his wife what a pale, gangly creature she'd been and how her naked body hadn't even been an enticement.

And that she hated almost more than anything else. That she had been so easily tricked by her emotions, by her passions. And that those passions had been so easily discarded.

Though, in this moment what she hated more was that she had allowed Nathan to have them.

She'd never looked at it quite the way Dmitri had presented it to her before. Certainly Nathan's interaction with her hadn't changed him one bit. It had changed his circumstances, but she was sure it hadn't changed him emotionally.

While she had contorted and rearranged everything she was because of him. In response to anger, in response to heartbreak and disgust, but nevertheless because of him.

If not for him, where would she be? The answer to that question had terrified her before, but now she was torn.

If he hadn't made her feel ashamed of her bare skin and everything beneath it, who would she be now?

There was something strange about this city that turned everything she thought and believed in on its head. There was something strange about this man who made her clothes feel too tight and made her heart feel too big for her chest.

Who could shrink her entire world down to the sensation of his thumb moving over the slick fabric of her top, his heat seeping through to her skin.

"You wish you were down there, don't you, Victoria?" His breath was hot on her neck, sending a shiver down her spine.

"No, I don't." And when she spoke the words she realized how true they were. She didn't want to be down there with them; she wanted to be right up here, so long as she was with him.

"What were you like before him?" The words were rough, sliding over her skin like a patch of velvet being rubbed the wrong way.

"I barely remember."

"Try." He tilted his head, and she felt the firm press of his mouth on the side of her neck. She stiffened, shock immobilizing her. Dimly, she thought that she should move away from him. That she should stop this madness before it progressed any further. But she didn't. She stayed rooted to the spot, held captive by her curiosity, by the desire to find out what he might do next.

"I was—" her voice was unsteady "—normal, I suppose. I wanted the same thing every teenager wants. To experience love and desire, to be wanted. I thought I found it, so I didn't examine it too closely. I was impetuous, and I led with my heart. And that I don't wish I could have back."

"What is it you wish you could have back?"

The word reverberated deep inside her, echoed in the empty chambers where it had once been. "Passion."

Somehow, just by saying it she felt as though she'd opened the door. As though she had broken locks that had been firmly closed for years.

He shifted their position slightly, tightening his hold on her, sliding his hand around to rest firmly on her stomach as he moved them both into the shadows of the balcony, so that she could just barely see the revelers through the twisting, twining ivy on the wrought-iron railings.

"I do not think you lost any of it. I think perhaps you might simply be sleeping."

"Do you think so?"

"I know how to wake you up."

All of the air rushed from her lungs. "How?"

"The only way to wake an enchanted princesses is with a kiss."

She should say no. She should tell him that he had taken the ruse too far, that she would never go back to being the girl she was, because she had learned far too much since then, and that girl was stupid. That he should understand because he knew that sometimes it was necessary to leave behind the old things. To let the old foolish self stay dead.

But she didn't do any of those things. Instead, she stood motionless as he swept his hand around to cup her cheek, his fingertips tracing lightly along the line of her jaw as he gently angled her head to face to the side.

As he bent down slowly—achingly so—his mouth now a whisper from hers.

She had plenty of time to turn away, plenty of time to tell him to stop. But she didn't.

Because for the first time in twelve years Victoria Calder was lost in passion, and she didn't want to be found.

The image of Nathan as he turned away from what she offered was blotted out by her need for Dmitri.

Instead of embracing her fear, her hard lessons learned, she tilted her chin upward and closed the distance between them, their mouths meeting abruptly. It was like touching a match to an oil slick, an inferno igniting between them that she never could've anticipated.

She had not kissed a man since Nathan. The closest she had come was Stavros a few years back, but it had felt nothing like this. The prelude hadn't held this much intensity, and she knew for a fact the kiss would never have been this explosive.

Dmitri groaned, deep and rough, the sound so wild it should've been unsettling. It wasn't. If anything, it added fuel to the flame, urging her on.

She raised her arm, resting her hand on the back of his neck, curling her fingers around his skin and holding him fast, parting her lips and deepening the kiss, letting her tongue slide against his.

Desire shot through her like an arrow, hitting its target straight and true between her thighs, sending an ache reverberating through her body.

Need, want, passion. Her mind was blank of anything else. She wanted nothing more than to continue to exist in this moment, nothing more at all. In this moment there were no department stores, there was no sin to be atoned for. There was only new sin to find and explore.

And she wanted to explore it all with him.

His fingertips slid up her stomach, teasing the underside of her breast before cupping it in his palm, squeezing her gently as though he was testing the weight of her. She wrenched her mouth away from his, a harsh groan on her lips. He released his hold on her face, lowering his hand to grip her hip, to pull her body back hard against his.

He was hot against her back, and she could feel his arousal hardening against her. She could not remember ever being so acutely aware of a man in this way, certainly not when she had kissed Nathan all those years ago. What she had done then had all been conducted with a girl's desire. She had wanted, but it'd been nebulous and vague. But right now she was a twenty-eight-year-old woman and she knew very well what she wanted. There was no misty veil drawn over her idea of sensuality and sex. No, Victoria was well aware of what went on between men and women. She had just never imagined she might want it, not like this.

She had intended to marry; she certainly had never intended to remain a virgin all these years, much less the rest of her life. But that was just one reason Stavros had been such a perfect pick. Not only because he was a prince, but because she felt nothing for him. Because her attraction to him had been almost nonexistent and therefore unchallenging. This had nothing to do with logic; this had nothing to do with bettering her position. This was all about feeling, all about need. All about every little thing she had spent years shunning and reducing in importance.

But she couldn't stop, not now. Even though the back of her mind was screaming that this was wrong, that she couldn't give in, her body was screaming louder. Her entire body demanded more.

He squeezed her breast again, dragging his thumb across one sensitized nipple before pinching her lightly between his thumb and forefinger. She flexed her hips, pressing her body more firmly against his hardening erection. She knew what she was asking for. And all she could do was pray that he would give it to her.

"Dmitri," she said, her voice husky, almost unrecognizable.

He responded, his words harsh, broken and in a foreign language. And though she couldn't understand what he was saying, she could understand exactly what he was doing. His hands sliding over her curves, ramping up her arousal, pushing her to the brink without even touching her beneath her clothes.

"Look at them down there," he said, pressing a kiss to her neck. "They think they are in the throes of ecstasy, that they are in the midst of the party. But they have no idea." He shifted, his hand moving between her thighs, the heel of his palm pressing against the center of her need. "If they looked up here they might. Do you think they could see?" The idea should have shocked her, but it didn't. Instead she found herself morbidly fascinated: Intrigued by the idea that the partiers could be watching her as she had watched them. That they might envy her, as she had once envied them. She did not now. Because Dmitri was holding her in his arms, so how could she wish to be anywhere else?

He applied gentle pressure between her thighs, sending a shot of pleasure straight to her core.

"If they could see you now," he continued, "they would see the most passionate creature in existence."

His words made her feel as if it might be true, that she wasn't hollowed out, that her passion hadn't been stolen from her. How could it have been? How could it have been when she was letting him hold her like this? When her entire body was crying out with need for him, with need for completion. Here on the balcony, out in the open, shrouded only by a few vines.

"But I'm glad they cannot see," he said, kissing her neck again. "I'm glad you're all mine. I'm glad this is only for me." His words should anger her, because she wasn't his. Instead, the roughly spoken claim in combination with the gentle rocking of his palm against the sensitized bundle of nerves was all it took to push her completely over the edge she hadn't even realized she'd been on.

She felt as if she was falling, over the balcony and down to the street below. Lights, sounds, swirled in her head, her mind empty of anything but the searing pleasure burning through her.

And when it passed, she was being held steady, still in Dmitri's arms. She hadn't fallen at all, because he had held her fast.

Then suddenly, it was as if her vision cleared. And she saw herself clearly. Saw this clearly. She was standing in the open on a balcony, and she had just let Dmitri bring her to orgasm. Dmitri, whom she had a business deal with. Dmitri, whom her entire future rode on. This was the one thing she could not afford to throw into jeopardy, and she had done just that by bringing something so volatile and personal into it.

She hadn't changed. She hadn't changed at all. When things became important, essential, she failed in the end.

All of the sweet, fuzzy pleasure that had been buzzing through her turned to ash, curling at the edges, folding in tightly on itself and wrapping her up tightly with it.

She pulled away from him, needing to put as much distance between the two of them as possible. She looked back down at Bourbon Street, at the people below. The hen party was gone. And she felt as if she could suddenly see everything down there for what it was. Nothing more than drunken excess. Sad people trying very hard to trick themselves into believing they were having fun.

It was nothing to aspire to. It was nothing to covet.

And she was a fool.

"I think I'll skip dessert." She ran her hands over her hair, desperately trying to straighten it, desperately trying to erase the evidence of what had just occurred. She started to walk away, her entire body beginning to shake.

"I think you already had dessert, Victoria."

She stopped, her body going stiff. "You bastard." She didn't turn around. She just kept walking.

And she vowed then and there that this wouldn't happen again. He was right—she had changed because of Nathan. But it was a change that had been for the better.

One thing she would not be doing was changing herself for Dmitri Markin.

CHAPTER SIX

DMITRI HAD SPENT the entire rest of the night lying awake, fighting a hard-on that wouldn't quit.

It was an interesting experience going to bed unsatisfied. And not only unsatisfied, but with a deep feeling of shame and failure that wrapped itself around the arousal, making it feel more potent, making it feel both worse and better at the same time.

Dmitri was very rarely rejected, if ever. When he wanted sex he was able to get it. Moreover, when he did not want sex he was able to resist it.

Somehow, neither of those things had happened last night.

He hadn't wanted to touch her, and yet he had. Then he had wanted her, and he had not got her.

He didn't know which was worse.

Today saw the harsh New Orleans sun shining brightly in the sky, and he had immediately decided to go for a run in the obstacle-ridden streets before going back to the suite to face both the day and his accomplice from last night. She had been sleeping when he left, but he knew she would be awake now. It was after nine, and Victoria seemed very much like the kind of person who was up with the birds. Especially when there was a project to be done, and today definitely had a list of projects to tackle.

He stepped into the living area that he and Victoria

shared just as Victoria was emerging from her bedroom.
She froze like a startled cat when she saw him, her hands
drawn up against her chest as though she were looking for
pearls to clutch.

She was not wearing pearls; a polka-dot dress fell down
past her knees, a wide patent leather belt highlighting her
narrow waist. The neckline was high, demure almost, as
all of her clothing seemed to be. And like the rest of her
clothing he found it unbearably sexy.

"Good morning," she said, her tone crisp.

"Yes, good morning."

She appraised his appearance, and clearly found him
wanting. Or at least, he was certain that was what she
wanted him to think. But he didn't miss the blush that
stained her cheeks as she took in the sight of him. "You
are not ready to go to the venue."

"Why? Will there be anyone there?"

"You are sweaty." She said it as though it was the most
distasteful thing she could even imagine.

"It's New Orleans. A quick jaunt outside and everyone
is sweaty."

"It looks like you've had more than a quick jaunt."

"I had some energy to burn off."

Tension crackled between them as he let the meaning
hit her fully. He shouldn't push her, because when he did
they ended up where they had ended up last night. And he
knew that he couldn't allow it to happen again. This did
not control him. There were so many paths he could take.
All roads did not lead to her.

"Did you?" she asked, her tone starchy. "I slept very well."

He let silence stretch between them. "Yes, I imagine
you did."

Her cheeks darkened a shade, and he could tell she was
thinking of last night. "I refuse to feel guilty about it."

"What about? That you managed to…get sleep when I didn't?"

"Yes." She elevated her chin and sauntered past him at a brisk pace, snatching her purse off the end table by the couch. "Shall we go?"

"The venue is here in the hotel, is it not?"

"Yes, it is."

"I am sweaty, as you said. Would you like to wait for me to rinse off?"

"I feel like we've played this game before. I would rather not be present every time you shower. We are just going downstairs, so your running clothes should be fine, and I will bear your sweat with as much grace and poise as I can."

"You are a consummate lady." He followed her out of the suite and into the hall.

"I do try to be."

She was so stiff and prim, but he knew better. And he would not allow her to pretend he didn't. "I especially admire the way you keep your composure as you come."

She whipped around to face him, her eyes wide with shock, her cheeks red now, not from embarrassment, but rage. "I cannot believe you mentioned that."

"I'm sorry. Were you dedicated to the idea of speaking about it in euphemism for the rest of our time together?"

"I had rather hoped we wouldn't speak of it at all."

"You were the one rather flagrantly flaunting your good night's sleep. And I'm the one who administered nature's sleeping pill—therefore, I think I have room to comment."

He shouldn't be discussing it, as he had just purposed that he would not press this issue with her. Because there was nowhere it could go.

But perhaps this was what he needed. Perhaps it was what they both needed. To allow a slight release on their control so that in all major areas that control could be retained.

It made sense. It was what he had done back when he was fighting MMA professionally. It had given him a chance to get release without ever descending back into the dark place he had been in. A chance to burn off steam while retaining the most essential elements of his control.

"That's crass." She pressed the button for the lift and proceeded to stare at the metal doors determinedly.

"Perhaps. But you did not seem to find it so distasteful last night."

"Until I could think again."

"I take that as a high compliment. The ability to make a woman like you mindless is not a small one."

She tilted her head to the side, her eyes narrowed, glittering with barely suppressed rage. "What's that supposed to mean?"

"Do not sound so offended, Victoria. It's a compliment." He examined the elegant line of her neck, a rush of desire coursing through his veins. "You are very present. Brilliant. Nothing gets past you. To force you to stop thinking for a moment shall be remembered as one of the greatest achievements of my life."

"Well, it shall go down in history as one of my biggest failures. Congratulations."

"Most women don't consider an orgasm of that quality a failure."

She made a frustrated sound and pressed the button for the lift again. "Honestly, it seems like this is taking forever."

"You're just saying that."

"So what is it you want, Dmitri?" she asked, the color high in her cheeks. "You just want to… What? Have sex?" Her prim and proper accent curving around that oh-so-

evocative word wrenched his arousal up to a higher level.
And he saw his paths narrowing. Saw his choices diminish. He should be angry, but his blood was burning with a
different kind of fire altogether. "We both know it won't
go anywhere. And we both know it might distract us from
what we have come together to do."

He reached out and took her left hand in his, sliding his
thumb over the ring that rested on her fourth finger. "I fail
to see how sex could do anything but enhance what it is
we are trying to do."

Why was he pushing this? Why was he letting this pull
to her, this situation he did not choose, dictate his wants,
his needs, his actions?

*Because you want to give in... This time at least, you
want to have the choice taken...*

"Oh, is that so?" Her voice sounded thin now, breathy.
Different.

Dammit all to hell. He wanted this. Wanted to pull the
trigger.

"We are supposed to be lovers, after all." He looked up,
his eyes clashing with hers. "Sex would add authenticity."

CHAPTER SEVEN

"I'M GOING TO choose to ignore that," Victoria said, her tone strangled, betraying just how affected she was by his bold statement.

The doors to the lift slid open and she called herself a whole list of vile names. She could not believe she was having this conversation with him, she could not believe she had let him touch her the way she had last night and, worst of all, she could not believe that she was tempted by what he was suggesting now.

She blamed... Well, she honestly had no idea what she blamed. Except for her own weakness. Apparently, she wasn't as strong as she'd imagined. Or, she had never been adequately tempted.

Not since Nathan. But even then...that had been different. It had been this hazy, romanticized thing. All bound up in fluttery feelings and breathless touches.

This was not fluttery. It was dark, sweaty and deep. Made her crave things she'd never imagined could possibly appeal.

Dmitri, it turned out, was her personalized brand of temptation. She was not sure how she felt about that.

She had always imagined that men like Nathan were her kryptonite. Men who talked a smooth game and wore well-fitted suits like a second skin.

And yet, here she was falling all over herself, breaking

vows that were more than a decade old, and all over a man who, when he wore a suit, looked as though he wanted to tear it from his body as soon as possible. A man who was rough, profane and seemed to take great joy in shocking her. A man who had access to parts of herself that were previously unknown. Parts of herself that wanted, craved, a chance to be wicked. To say to hell with everyone and everything else and dive into her own desires. Her own pleasures. A man who had thought nothing of touching her intimately on a balcony where anyone could see.

And you let him...

Well, that was beside the point. Or maybe it was exactly the point. She didn't know.

Dmitri got next to her in the lift, and the door slid shut. She felt as if she could barely breathe. And if she did breathe, she was certain she would inhale the scent of him, of his skin, of his sweat, and she knew full well that did not have the effect on her that she wished it did. She wished that it disgusted her. When she had walked into his gym only a few short weeks ago she had been filled with disdain for testosterone. Now she found it all much more appealing than she would like.

The elevator stopped on the ground floor and the doors opened. Victoria stepped down, not waiting for Dmitri, desperate for some distance. Of course, she had a feeling that as large as the continent was she wouldn't have enough distance from him if she was on an opposite coast. Better if she were back in England and he were here.

"The ballroom is this way," she said, without looking back at him. She could hear his heavy footfalls behind her, and more than that, she could sense his presence.

She led him down the hallway, her shoes loud on the marble floor. In contrast, his trainers kept him almost silent, and made her increasingly self-conscious. It wasn't fair—he should be the one feeling self-conscious, as he was in athletic clothing and casual shoes. Alas. Dmitri never seemed to feel uncomfortable, even though he never quite fit in to his surroundings. He simply didn't care. She had no idea how he managed such a thing.

She had no idea how he managed much of what he seemed to manage. Least of all his ability to reach into her and take control of her desire.

She had lost herself completely last night, and she would love to blame the city, she would love to blame the wine, but she knew it was him. Because the changes had started long before they had left England. They had started the moment she had walked into his gym and seen him standing there, looking like a bare-chested warrior from another age.

And she had thought herself immune because she had imagined he wouldn't be her type. It was laughable.

Another issue with having not had much experience with men since she was a girl. Victoria the woman obviously had no use for the smooth sophisticate. Which made no sense, since she fancied herself a smooth sophisticate, and one would think that she would be attracted to the sort of man whose lifestyle was compatible with hers.

Nothing about Dmitri would be compatible with her lifestyle and the long term.

But who's thinking about the long term?

No, she silenced that treacherous voice in her head. She was not going to allow herself to lose her sanity that way.

Who was she kidding? Her sanity was gone. There was no other way to look at it. Thinking about his footsteps in relation to hers, and how well he fit into his surroundings or, rather, how well he didn't? And obsessing about the sound of her own shoes?

She had to stop obsessing about *him*.

So he had given her an orgasm. It wasn't as though she'd never given herself one.

And when she did, it wasn't as if she went around thinking about it all day after the fact, either. There was no reason she should think about it so much just because someone else had done it. It wasn't as though they'd had sex. He'd touched her—that was all.

And kissed her, and caressed her in ways no other man ever had.

But still, all of it was irrelevant. She needed to keep her focus. She needed to think about what was important and that was the gala that was happening tonight.

She walked through the elegant double doors at the end of the hall and gestured for Dmitri to follow.

"I think this will do," she said.

"Do you?"

"I do." She was irritated, and it wasn't really warranted. But, oh well. She was feeling annoyed, even if he wasn't deserving of the irritation in question. "Yes, this is the venue. If you have a negative opinion about it I suggest you keep it to yourself. If you wanted to choose, then you should have done so."

"I did not say I didn't like it," he said.

"You had a tone," she said, her tone clipped.

"Did I?" He chuckled, and she was really starting to hate when he did that, because she could not hear it and remain unaffected. "I didn't know you were so in tune to the changes in my voice inflection, *milaya moya*."

"I am not, and you can spare me your foreign endearment." Even *she* was annoyed with her responses at the moment, but she couldn't seem to hold them back. He had too much power over her. Over how she felt.

"They aren't foreign to me."

She bristled, feeling very much as if he had the upper

hand, and there was nothing she could do to reverse their roles. "Fair point."

"Yes, this will do nicely. I gather you're expecting a good turnout tonight?"

This was her area of strength; this was her confidence. The upper hand was here, and she was grabbing it. "That I am, Dmitri. That I am."

"You should be very proud. All you have to do is beat a few bushes and celebrities fall out. I would wager that would not be the case for me."

Because she was better with people than he was. And better at this. And that thought cheered her immensely. "You don't think?"

"No, I do not think. Unless said celebrity wanted to install a cage in the midst of a gala and arrange a fight, then have me seduce his wife, I fail to see why I would be included in something of this nature. That's what I am, after all. That's why my reputation is what it is."

She looked at Dmitri, his broad shoulders and well-defined muscles tapering down to a slim waist. The way the slight bump in his nose added to the look of him, to the danger. He certainly wouldn't blend in at a social event like this one, but then, there was something nice about not blending in. At least when it applied to other people. She had always gone out of her way to blend in as best she could.

"You're more than that," she said, and she wasn't sure why.

"Do you think?" he asked. "I'm not certain. But we had better make everyone think so, yes?"

She nodded slowly. "Yes." She cleared her throat. "So, there will be tables and chairs set over here. Dinner will be served around nine, then it will be dancing and live jazz music. It sounds nice, doesn't it?" She was desperate to change the subject, to get things back on track. To ignore all of the electricity that crackled between them.

"You're avoiding looking at me, Victoria."

She kept her eyes fixed on the stage. "I am not avoiding looking at you, Dmitri. It's just I can look at you anytime, and we came down here to look at the venue. I don't see why I should need any of this special, allotted venue time to examine you."

He made a low, musing noise in the back of his throat, and the hair on her neck stood on end. "And you are acting prickly. You're prickly when things don't go your way." He started to pace the length of the room. "I have been perfectly agreeable, so I know it is not myself making you feel like things aren't going your way. Which makes me wonder…is your body disobeying you, Victoria?"

She stiffened. "Why would you think that?"

"I only wonder if your body is still obeying *me*."

Oh, that…

She made a sound that was somewhere between a snort and a growl. "I have no idea what that's supposed to mean. At no point has my body ever obeyed yours."

"Last night," he said, the words dark and sensual, wrapping themselves around her body. No. No, no, no.

She gritted her teeth. Part of her was begging her to retreat, while the bolder part, the part that hated to lose, that seemed to be in top form when he was around, urged her on. "Stop feeling so proud. It's nothing I haven't done for myself."

He arched a dark brow. "On a balcony in front of the sea of strangers? You are a much more adventurous woman than I have given you credit for."

She ignored the heat sizzling beneath her skin. "We are not going to talk about this again. We are going to talk about the gala tonight."

"All right, Victoria, we can play your way. But before we do, I have one question for you."

"What?" She braced herself mentally for what he might say.

He was silent for a while, the silence winding itself around the line of tension that already stretched between them and pulling it tight. Finally, he spoke. "Do you want me? Do you want more than what happened last night?"

"I don't see what that has to do with anything." Being curt was her last line of defense. And even it was hanging on by a thread.

"It doesn't matter if it's relevant or not, this is what I'm asking you right now. I told you, one question. And then we can get back to being relevant."

She took in a deep breath, deciding yet again that she was going to pursue honesty. Because after what had transpired between them the night before it would be foolish of her to try and deny that there was something between them. Ignoring it wasn't working anyway. "*Obviously*, I am attracted to you. It would be disingenuous of me to say otherwise. As to the question of whether or not I *want* you, that's a different story."

"Is it? Do you think wanting me and *wanting* to want me are the same?"

She felt some of the defenses around her crumble. "Aren't they?"

He looked at her, his dark eyes boring into hers. She could feel frustration coming off him in waves. "No, Victoria, they are not the same thing. I could go out onto the street, snap my fingers and have any woman I wanted—do you realize that? I can go right outside this hotel this very moment and find a woman and be back in my room having sex with her in less than an hour. I have that choice." His voice vibrated with intensity, an intensity that echoed through her. "But…I don't want to make it. Because I want *you*." The words hit her hard, unexpected and, much more unexpected than the words themselves, welcome.

He wanted her.

He wanted *her*.

Not because of what she could offer him, but because he was attracted to her. He already had use of her, without seduction. This had to do with lust. Simple lust. And it meant more to her than she'd ever imagined something like that might.

He continued. "Do you suppose I find that terribly convenient? Do you suppose I want that? No, I would much rather have the easy way. What man wouldn't? But with us, it will never be simple."

Victoria's throat constricted, her chest tightening. "Why bother with something that isn't easy?" she asked. "I mean…isn't life hard enough?"

"True," he said, his voice rough. "But easy is never fun. Not for people like us."

The truth that resonated, in his words and through her, was unwelcome. "I would take some easy," she contradicted.

He met her gaze. "No. You don't want easy. You're like me. You want a fight. You want this fight, too, don't you?"

"Fine," she said, barely able to force the words out. "Fine, I want you. But I don't want to want you." She finished the rest of it in a rush, not quite able to believe she'd said it out loud.

She felt as though she had stuck her head into a bonfire. She'd done this once before. And she'd been rejected horribly, seen her entire life turned upside down because she'd chased after desire. She had laid herself bare and been turned away, and even saying those words to Dmitri now took her right back to that place. To feeling as though she'd taken her clothes off for him to either accept or reject. Just as she'd done back then. But this was more somehow, bigger, even without all of the feelings that had accompanied her attempted seduction of Nathan.

Because it had been one thing to offer herself to a man when she'd been a sixteen-year-old girl who had wanted something nebulous and romantic. Who had wrapped everything in the soft haze of love and fine feelings.

It was quite another thing to say it to a man like Dmitri. When what she wanted had nothing to do with romance or love. When it had everything to do with desire. When she was a woman and old enough to understand exactly what that meant. To know that the ache between her thighs was because she was desperate to be filled by him, that she wanted him inside of her, skin to skin, clinging to each other as they both chased their climax.

She felt dizzy, her vision getting fuzzy around the edges, the world tilting on its axis.

"I will not seduce you," he said, his voice rough, "you have my word."

She laughed shakily. "As if you could seduce me."

"I already have, Victoria. I think I proved that last night. I said I enjoyed having you mindless, and I did. But the truth is I do not want you mindless when I finally take you to bed. I want you to know exactly what you're getting into. I want you to know exactly what you are agreeing to when you say *yes, Dmitri, yes*. So I will not seduce you. You will choose it. You will beg me," he said, his tone rough, harsh, his dark eyes blazing.

This was not the laid-back playboy she'd met, casually sparring with a man in the gym. This was the warrior. And for the first time she truly appreciated what he was.

And it only enticed her further.

"I would not…" She tried to force words through her dry throat. "I will not…"

"If you will not, then we will not. I will not push it." He unbound the leather cuff that was tied around his wrist. She had noticed it on their first meeting and a couple of times since. It had stood out because he was a man who didn't seem to care about his appearance one way or another, which meant it wasn't just a simple accessory. He took it in his hands, then held it out toward her. "Take this."

She closed the distance between them and took it, running her fingers over the leather, still warm from the contact with his skin.

Everything about him made her warm.

"What is this?" she asked.

"This is something that I always wore when I fought. It's kind of a good luck charm. It has no real sentimental significance. I wore it in fights." His tone was detached, as though he was speaking well-rehearsed lines that were meant for someone else. "I don't fight anymore. I only wear it out of habit. It's yours now."

There was something more. Something he wasn't telling her. And yet she felt she had no right to question him. Because she shouldn't care.

But she found she did.

"Why?" she asked. "Why are you giving this to me? To make me feel indebted to you? If so, I must tell you it will take more than a leather bracelet to accomplish that."

"That isn't the idea. I feel in debt to *you*. You gave something to me last night."

Her heart pounded wildly, and she wondered for a moment if he had guessed. If he had known that he was the first man to ever give her an orgasm. If he had figured out that she was a virgin. That would be a humiliation too many.

"What is it I gave you?" she asked.

"Your release, princess. I consider that a gift." He reached out and touched the end of the cuff, avoiding her skin. "I'm giving this to you with no expectation. It makes us even. However—" his eyes met hers, and a sharp shock of pleasure hit her low and square in the stomach "—if you would like to be with me all you have to do is return this." He lowered his hand and took a step back.

She swallowed hard, drawing her hands to her chest, holding the cuff tight. "Why?"

"Nathan seduced you. You were young, and he took advantage of that. If you and I are together I want to know it's your choice. I want to know for sure that it's because you want to be with me. That you have made a decision to be with me. This will prove it."

She curled her fingers around the strap. "Well, you won't be getting it back, so I really hope you weren't lying about it having no sentimental value attached to it."

"I wasn't. That is your decision. I will not take it from you. As I said, if you want me, you will have to give it to me. I know what it is like to be left with no choice. I find nothing attractive about forcing a woman into my bed. Force by tricking someone, by stripping their options, threatening them…all of it is the same to me. I know what it's like. To have the impossible before you. A moment that changes everything. That wrenches your choices right from your hands. I will not do the same to you. You have my word."

And suddenly, Dmitri turned and walked out of the room, leaving her standing there clutching the leather bracelet.

She looked down at it, the symbol of her choice that he had placed in her hand. And she tightened her grasp. She was going to resist this. She had to. If she didn't, she would have no one to blame but herself.

CHAPTER EIGHT

EVERYTHING WAS GOING according to plan—the tables were set perfectly, an elegant dinner laid out before exceedingly happy guests. Victoria was thrilled with the outcome of the gala, and with the turnout. The one thing she was less than thrilled about was Dmitri. Not because he hadn't dressed the part, but because he had, and so convincingly. He was almost a stranger tonight in a well-fitted tux that molded so perfectly to his masculine physique it had clearly been made for him.

His tattoos were covered, his muscles only hinted at, and yet, he still didn't appear quite tame. She was glad she could see the hint of wildness because civilized Dmitri was off-putting. She didn't know why he was off-putting, only that he was. She had become strangely attached to the surly, feral man she had spent the past couple of days with. The man who had kissed her, touched her out on the balcony last night.

She thought of her clutch purse, sitting in the cloakroom, containing the leather cuff Dmitri had given her earlier. She intended to hold on to it forever.

So why she had brought it with her into the ballroom she had no idea. Because she wouldn't be needing it. Because she would not be returning it to him.

But you want to.

She bit down hard on the inside of her cheek, hoping to

cool the arousal that was pouring through her body. She couldn't dwell on this. Could not give in to the attraction she felt for him.

She also did her best to ignore the sound of her shoes on the marble floor. Her rather saucy high heels that she'd never given a second thought to before Dmitri.

Shoes that begged a man to bend her over furniture, he'd said.

No.

She did her best to ignore the voice that was growing increasingly louder inside of her. The voice that was starting to question her resoluteness. Starting to wonder why it would be such a bad idea to just give in to what she wanted.

Because, the more sensible part of her answered, *I've spent too long forcing myself into this mold to break out of it now.*

Well, that sounded like her. Clinging to something out of sheer bloody-mindedness and no other reason.

What about fear? Is fear a good enough reason?

Yes, she had decided fear was a good enough reason. And she ignored the kick of disappointment in her gut as she reaffirmed her decision. She was keeping the leather cuff with her. He was never getting it back. Good luck charm or not. The slight twinge of guilt she felt about it was ridiculous, because that was why he had given her the cuff in the first place. She was certain of it. To make her feel guilty, to make her feel as if she should give it back, rather than holding on to it because of what it was, not because of what she wanted.

Of course, that wasn't how he'd said it.

Leaving the decisions entirely up to her, now that she thought about it, was the worst part. Because if she indulged herself, she was to blame. Because if she deprived herself, it was because of her. And she couldn't blame anyone else. It was the only good thing about Nathan, and the incident with him.

She'd been sixteen, and while she took her share of the blame, rerouting her entire life based on her mistake, she logically knew that a good portion of the fault lay with him. Because he had been adult. Because she'd had no experience with men.

She hadn't realized until this moment, standing in a crowded ballroom, just how much blame she *did* allow Nathan to bear. And how that blame spared her a good portion of the pain she would feel otherwise.

It made her wonder if what really held her back was fear. Fear of rejection. That she might take her clothes off for a man again and see nothing but pity. See that while he'd wanted to use her, he didn't really want her body at all.

That there was something wrong with her, with it. With everything she was inside and out.

She couldn't stand that.

She took a deep breath. This was not the time to be thinking about that. She had to circulate. More importantly, she had to find her fiancé and circulate with him.

She looked across the ballroom and saw him standing next to a table with a tray of champagne positioned on it, looking out of place.

There he was, the Dmitri she knew. He looked too large for the space, too wild. And that was precisely what drew her to him.

She started to cross the room and he looked up, meeting her eyes. He schooled his expression into one of perfect civility and leaned back against the wall, waiting for her to come to him, his movements fluid like a panther. Or more terrifying, like a banker. When she made her way to where he was, he didn't speak, instead taking her hand in his and lowering his head to kiss her knuckles.

She took a deep breath, trying to keep herself from focusing too intently on the press of his lips against her skin. On what it had felt like to have his lips touch her other places. She cleared her throat. "Who are you? And what have you done with Dmitri?"

He released her hand. "Are you not pleased?"

"I'm pleased. You look every inch the suave sophisticate. How can I not be pleased?"

"You do not seem pleased."

She lifted her shoulder. "I'm possibly a little bit confused. You seem different."

"Because I'm not shirtless and dripping with sweat?"

She swallowed hard. "Perhaps. Perhaps it is that." It was, partly. Because the wilder parts of him were so well concealed right now, and she rather admired those parts.

Not because they matched her in any way, but because they so weren't her. Because they were so far from her reality. They were like everything good and lush. Refreshing in a dry wasteland of parties, crystalline conversation and self-denial, of which she had grown exceedingly weary.

Just then she felt very tired. Tired of being good. Tired of the long road to atonement. Tired of being afraid.

Tired, quite frankly, of being a virgin.

She would do anything right at this moment to go back to the moment on the balcony when his hand had skimmed over her curves and she had felt nothing but desire. When she had felt no guilt, no trepidation, nothing but need. When the voices in her head had been completely blocked out in favor of the heat that was coursing through her body.

And her mind was back on the cuff that was in the cloakroom in her bag.

No.

"So—" she snagged a glass of champagne from the nearby tray "—how do you find the party so far?"

"It is going well. I'm not particularly looking forward to giving my speech, but I feel prepared."

"You are prepared." Much more prepared than she had imagined he could be for something like this.

"And you look surprised."

"I am, perhaps, a little bit surprised."

"Don't be—this was your idea."

She looked away from him. "I suppose my surprise comes from the fact that you listened to me."

"Well, I did enlist your services. And your hand."

She lifted her hand, causing the yellow diamond on her finger, which she was starting to like, to glisten in the light. "More like I enlisted yours," she said.

"But I agreed that you could be of use."

"Oh. That's nice. I'm of use," she said, lowering her hand.

"Not exactly the use I'm hoping for yet."

"Stop," she said, ignoring the flush of pleasure that went through her. She should be angry at him. She should not find him sexy.

The music stopped playing, and the emcee running the event went to the front of the room and started doing an introduction for Dmitri.

For some reason her stomach went tight. It wasn't possible she was nervous for him, was it?

No, not that. She was nervous because she needed it to go well. Because he needed to say the right thing, or else all of this would be pointless. She was here to help him, and she really did want this to succeed. She didn't like failing, even when the cause wasn't hers.

Dmitri downed the rest of his champagne quickly, then set the glass down on the table next to them. Unthinkingly, she reached up and straightened his tie, her fingertips brushing his skin just above his shirt collar, sending lightning shooting through her. She cleared her throat. "You'll do fine."

A smile curved his lips, and yet she could see that he was strained. "Of course I will. I win every fight I step into."

He walked away from her toward the front of the room, taking his position on the stage. And then he began to speak.

"I would like to thank you all for coming here tonight. I would like to thank most especially my beautiful fiancée, Victoria Calder, for arranging such a civilized event. If left to my own devices you would all be eating cocktail weenies from a buffet." That line elicited laughter from the audience. "I am not known for my sophistication and manners—that much is true. What I am best known for is my fighting. Times have changed for me—my life has changed. But what has not changed is the foundation I was built on. Things that I learned under the mentorship of Colvin Davis. A native of New Orleans, Colvin came to London to change his fortune, then he traveled to Russia looking for champion fighters and found...me. A disappointment, I would think. But he saw my potential. What happened after that changed life for both of us." He shifted his position at the podium, and Victoria held her breath, willing him to keep talking. To keep going. To keep fighting. She could see his discomfort, but she imagined the audience didn't. He had a good mask. But she knew him well enough to see beyond it. When had that happened? And why?

He continued. "The values he instilled in me were the values that enabled me to become not only an award-winning fighter, but a successful businessman. He gave me control when I had none. He helped me manage my anger when anger was all I had. He gave me life when before all I had was survival. This is what I want to offer the children who come to the gyms I hope to establish with this charity. A place with mentors, a place for them to learn patience. To learn to protect themselves. And the values to know when to use it. An important part of martial arts is the control you learn along with it, and it is that control that changed my life. I hope you will allow me to pass this on to others. I hope you will allow me to change life for these children the way it was changed for me. I hope you will be moved to give generously."

It was completely silent in the room, not even the sound of clinking cutlery on plates breaking the reverie that had settled over them. "I know my reputation has not always been exemplary. I have enjoyed my fame, my money. Coming from poverty, having access to so many new things…it turned my head. But Colvin brought me from the darkness, and without him I would not be here standing before you. And without Victoria Calder I would not be here tonight." He gestured toward her and all eyes were now on her. She smiled, easily, never finding it a challenge to play to a crowd. And yet, this felt different. This was affecting something in her chest, making her feel *things*. For him. And she would use it now. Use it to make this look real. He was lying now, giving her credit where none was due, and he was doing it to lend validity to a charity that was coming from his heart, not hers. She wouldn't fail him now. It seemed essential somehow. As if this moment was pivotal. As if it somehow overshadowed the mistakes of the past, the present large and full, more important than it had been in years. With the past looming large and the future her hope, *now* was so often lost. But not in this moment.

"It is she who inspired me to take what assisted me in bringing it to the world. She who inspired me to use my gifts to help others. I will stop boring you now. Enjoy your dinner, enjoy your dancing, enjoy your evening."

There were applause and Dmitri walked down from the stage, making a beeline for the back of the room, and for her.

Victoria was about to say something to him, about to compliment him on his performance, when the band began to play again.

He did not let her speak. Instead, he extended his hand to her. She took it and she found herself being drawn in close to his body.

"And now, my dearest fiancée," he said, "I think you should dance with me."

She should have been the one to suggest dancing, considering she was supposed to be the bastion of manners and grace. She had not expected for Dmitri to be the one to make that overture. But then, she had not expected he could look so good in a suit. So, he seemed to be offering up surprises all over the place.

She smiled, acutely aware that all eyes were on them. "Of course."

She allowed him to lead her out to the center of the dance floor, forced herself to relax against his body as he pulled her into his arms. Her breath caught as he leaned in, his breath fanning over her cheek. "I should like to avoid as much social interaction as possible."

She let out a nervous laugh, strangely disappointed by the fact that his asking her to dance was merely a diversion. Because he had made such a romantic statement in his speech, she had no doubt that they would not be interrupted out here on the dance floor. People would be content to simply watch them lost in their apparent bubble of love.

"A room with five hundred people may not be the best venue for solitude."

He placed his hand on her lower back, tightening his hold on her. "Perhaps. But this is what we came here to do, isn't it?" he asked.

"And so far, I think we have done it very well." She didn't know why, but she wanted to reassure him. Perhaps because she knew that giving the speech had been outside his comfort zone, and yet he had done it.

"A compliment?"

"Don't sound so surprised."

Their dancing was little more than swaying to the music while holding each other, and she found it slightly disconcerting. Because it seemed rather less like dancing as an activity and rather more like something people chose to do if they wanted to touch each other in public and could not think of another socially acceptable way to accomplish that.

"You have a way of taking a tone that sounds a bit like a disapproving schoolmistress."

"Not the sort of mistress I'm supposed to appear to be."

"I think not." He lifted his hand and cupped her chin between his thumb and forefinger. "You're supposed to appear to be the sort of mistress who warms my bed, not one who sends me to bed alone without supper."

"It's a good thing that we are putting on a very convincing show, then," she said, looking away from him to try to gauge the reactions of those still sitting at the tables. He tightened his grip on her chin, preventing her from keeping her focus away from him.

"Perhaps you should give me a kiss."

Her heart slammed against her chest. "I thought you weren't going to seduce me."

"I'm not." He slid his thumb along the outer edge of her lower lip. "I am simply keeping up appearances."

She suddenly became acutely aware of her mouth, and her lips felt exceedingly dry. She hadn't been aware of that at all only a moment ago, and now it was all she could think about. That she needed badly to moisten her lips. Ridiculous. And she felt too self-conscious to do it. Even more ridiculous.

Still, she found herself running her tongue along the surface of her lower lip, then her upper lip. He shifted his thumb higher, and something wicked overtook her, something that she would not have ever said lurked inside of her, not even at her deepest, most hidden depths. But apparently, it did. She stuck her tongue out again, letting the edge of it touch his thumb, the sharp tang of salt from his skin a force that rocked her body.

Their eyes clashed and held. "Do you know what you are inviting?"

She nodded slowly. "I think I do."

She raised her hand to touch his face, and he caught it, pulling it back down to her side. "You can't be asking for sex, darling. Because you have not given me what I require."

Her breath caught. Of course. That little leather wristband that would signify her freely given choice. That would have to be given to him in a thinking moment, not a feeling moment. That would drastically cool the heat between them, giving her time to reconsider. And he knew that, which was why he had done it. She chose to see clearly now and without ulterior motive. Just now she was opting to look at it at face value.

"We have to stay for another hour." They could not leave any earlier than that—it was impossible. "The leather cuff is in my purse, which is in the cloakroom. I'm going to give it to you on our way out." Her words were rushed, and she could barely believe she had spoken them even after they had left her mouth. Could hardly believe that she was committing to this.

But why not? *Why not?* Nothing she had ever done so far had been able to atone for the sins of her past. She had been good; she had been the best daughter she could possibly be. She had not caused any trouble, had dated no one but a prince in the ensuing years since her one very bad decision. And what had it got her? Nothing. At least, nothing for her. But here she was now on the cusp of her redemption, knowing that the return of London Diva would restore her to the proper place in her family. And knowing for sure that nothing else would.

She had let one man destroy her feelings about her body, her sex, her feelings. Had let him ruin her relationship with her father.

Then she had hidden every part of herself she'd decided was wrong and had sought to prove to her father that she had moved past her youthful mistakes, had sought to prove to herself that she was smarter, stronger.

But in the end her father didn't care about that. He didn't care whether or not she got the business back by striking a business deal, or by trading her body. He would never have cared if she had married a prince, or merchant. He would never forgive her, not really. He would never see her the way that he once had.

That was all very clear to her now.

No one cared but her. Everyone had moved on but her.

And with that strange feeling of sadness and freedom roaring through her, she knew her decision had been made. There was no future with Dmitri. But she was okay with that. She didn't need a future with him; she just needed a future for herself. One that wasn't for her father, one that wasn't in response to Nathan.

She would start tonight. With this decision. With this

step forward. Reclaiming something that she would have had long ago if she hadn't allowed her mistake to define her.

"Be very certain," he said.

"Do I strike you as someone who doesn't know her mind, Dmitri?" she asked, raising a brow and keeping her tone arch.

"No."

"I thought not."

"And now we only have to wait an hour."

Her stomach constricted, but it wasn't nerves having their way with her right now. No, it was excitement. Lust. Lust that she was finally, for the first time, embracing.

"Yes," she said, "an hour."

CHAPTER NINE

THE HOUR DMITRI had to endure after Victoria made her shaky promise was interminable. In a fight, in the ring, time seemed to move both slower and faster. Minutes could stretch out into eternity and the final seconds end as though they had never existed. Nights spent in his family's posh home when he'd been growing up had been unremarkable. The nights after his exile spent on the gritty streets had been another thing entirely.

Dmitri was accustomed to the relativity of time.

Still, he had never experienced it on quite this level before. Every moment of small talk would have been torture regardless of what had passed between Victoria and him, but this brought it to new heights. It was all but impossible to focus on what some celebrity in a monkey suit was saying, when in his mind he was already imagining what it would be like to take hold of the zipper on the red dress Victoria was wearing and draw it down, watch the rich fabric part to reveal lily-white skin beneath.

When he was already picturing what it would be like to slide into her tight wet heat, to be skin to skin with her, to feel her tremble beneath his touch. Yes, as torturous as small talk seemed on a good day, it was amplified in this moment.

He looked down at his watch, at the bare spot above it where the leather strap was usually tied. And he breathed a sigh of relief when the minute hand ticked over and the timer on this particular fight was up.

Now he had another one stretching before him. And this one, he had the feeling would go by much too quickly.

There was nothing he could offer Victoria beyond tonight, or perhaps beyond a physical relationship that would extend only until their business dealings were done.

Either way, the timer had started already.

He abruptly broke away from the man who was speaking to him, knowing that he appeared rude, and not giving a damn. He had one thing on his mind now, and that was Victoria. Victoria and her lovely body, Victoria and her lovely lips. Victoria and her crisp, crystal voice and the opportunity to shatter it yet again as he brought her to the peak of pleasure.

He made his way through the ballroom, over to where she stood. Her blond hair was captured in a low bun at the nape of her neck that had been left loose, some curls escaping and cascading down her back, which was revealed to perfection by the cut of the red gown she was wearing that exposed the elegant line of her spine. The high neck of the front provided the tease, which he was starting to believe Victoria was a master of. Revealing just enough, concealing even more.

In both her wardrobe and in her interactions.

An irresistible combination.

"Victoria," he said, watching the color in her cheeks darken as he approached. "I believe, my love, it is time for us to go." He looked at the group of people she was engaged in conversation with. "Unless, you find yourself more occupied here."

"Of course not. What could I possibly find more engaging than spending an evening with you?" The way she spoke the words was flirtatious, calculated. Designed to add to the illusion of their relationship, designed to give them both an escape, and designed to leave the people she had been conversing with unoffended. "You understand, don't you?" She asked the question with a hint of cheekiness that left no doubt in anyone's mind as to why they were escaping.

Following her lead, he winked and said something in Russian, something bland that had more to do with the weather than with seduction, but the people in Victoria's group had no clue. They smiled, and the women exchanged looks, the kind that let him know if he wanted to pursue them at some point, they would be open to it.

Too bad for them he only had eyes for Victoria.

He wrapped his arm around Victoria's waist and pulled her close to him. "We can't forget to make a stop at the cloakroom first."

"No, indeed." She offered a wave to those standing near them and then curled herself into his side, her body much more tense than it undoubtedly appeared to the onlookers

"You are not having second thoughts, are you?" he asked.

"Why would you ask that?"

"Because right now you are holding yourself with all of the tension of a woman going to the gallows, not to bed with a lover."

"You have to bear with me. I'm not very experienced."

That made his stomach tighten, guilt gnawing in him. Of course she wouldn't be very experienced. She had been badly burned by her first lover. She would have been very cautious in every situation since then. And he could hardly blame her. Likely, she was a woman who had relationships, and none of these no-strings sexual encounters. All of it cut a bit too close to the bone for him. Because he was jaded, he could admit. He was the sort of man who had encounters like this all the time. With women who were accustomed to having them.

They cost him nothing; it cost his lovers nothing. Not a moment's worth of worry even. It made him feel guilty to know that she was worried now, but not enough that he would turn back. Because, while he still had a conscience left to burn, it was on life support. And it had very little say in the ultimate outcome of what he did.

He really was a bastard.

He did not deserve to put his hands on her. Rough, tattooed, fighter's hands, stained with ink, stained with blood. The man he'd been…the boy he'd been before his world had changed forever could have been good enough for her. But he had not been allowed to remain that boy. He'd been forced to change, to adapt. And he had.

He'd been pushed into violence, and so he'd become violent.

In contrast, she was smooth, untouched by the world in many ways. And he knew it. There would be no pretending later. He knew what he was doing. And more importantly he knew what he would not be able to do for her after. He could offer her nothing. Nothing but this.

But, though it should, it was not going to stop him.

"You have nothing to fear from me," he said, feeling as if he was telling her a lie. "I have no desire to hurt you." That much was true, though it might be inevitable.

"I won't turn back. I've made up my mind." They paused in front of the door of the coat check, and Victoria handed the woman sitting at the front her numbered ticket. A black wrap and handbag appeared a moment later, and Victoria wasted no time in opening up the little clutch and producing the cuff he'd given her this morning.

She extended her hand and placed it into his with trembling fingers. "See? I'm committed. I'm making this decision while not under the influence of lust. Well, not *mind-numbing* lust anyway. You aren't talking me into it while you have me in a fog. We had the hour. We had this long walk over here. We even had this little talk about my nerves. And the answer is still yes. This cuff is still yours. And I still want you."

He had told her that the leather cuff he wore around his wrist meant nothing. He had lied. It was his father's. And he had taken it off the man's dead body in the moments after his life had exploded around him.

A reminder.

Of the fact that he was a changed man now, because his father had pushed him to decide between two impossible things: his life, or Dmitri's and his mother's.

Of the fact that truly, there had been only one choice. It was only a matter of being strong enough to make it.

And he was.

He began to tie the cuff back around his wrist, just above his watch. "You have no idea how much this pleases me, *milaya moya.*"

He realized his hands were shaking, too. There was something happening inside of him, a kind of shivering sensation taking him over. It was not like anything he'd felt before.

The closest it came was to the moment just before he had taken that gun in his hands in a beautiful home in Moscow and pointed it at the man that he had always called father. He had felt something like this then. As though the control was slipping away from his grasp, as though everything was about change. As though life and death hung in the balance and if he did not make a decision quickly he would fall on the wrong side of it. As though all of life's options had reduced down to one, one that was terrible, great, powerful and unavoidable.

Yes, this strange trembling feeling was most comparable to that.

To fear.

But that was crazy. What man feared a naked woman? Certainly not him. He had seen countless naked women before, had put his hands on them. Had been inside of them. Why should she be different?

Because she is.

And he had known that from the beginning, which was why he had taken great pains to avoid this. To avoid touching her, kissing her, *wanting* her. Because he had known even then that she was different. That this was different.

Ridiculous. She might be different, but she was still just a woman.

He gritted his teeth and turned to face her. "Shall we go?"

"Yes, happily, we are already sharing a room so that takes away some of the awkwardness of the whole your-room-or-mine question."

"We do not have the same bedroom in the suite."

"Still, it eliminates the walk of shame risk."

"Victoria," he said.

"What?"

"Stop talking."

She snapped her mouth shut, her crimson lips sealed tightly. He was tempted to make a dry comment about how rare this must be, but he refrained. This was not the time for jokes.

She had been making them to clear the tension, and he had decided he did not want any of it diminished. He wanted this moment. All of it. All of her.

He wrapped his arm around her waist and walked them both down the corridor that led to the elevators. He pressed the button and waited in silence before they stepped inside, finding themselves shrouded in the relative privacy.

Under normal circumstances he would immediately close the distance between himself and his prospective lover. Would pull her into his arms and began what would be finished in the bedroom right here on the way.

But not here. Not now, not with Victoria.

He only wanted to look at her for a while. To watch the pulse beat at the base of her throat, to watch the faint blush in her cheeks spread over the rest of her skin, flesh that spoke of arousal. To see the blue of her eyes all but disappear as her pupils expanded, as her eyes darkened.

To appreciate the fact that he still didn't know what she looked like naked. To savor this time of not knowing, because soon every question would be answered.

There was something perversely pleasurable about this moment of in between. This last bit of torture. Of not having, of wanting. Of being so near to satisfaction he could taste it, but far enough that he was in near physical pain from the weight of resisting.

Victoria took a deep breath, her shoulders lifting slightly, her fingers tightening on the little clutch bag she was still holding. She was nervous. But she was also excited. He had never fully appreciated how enjoyable it could be to watch for these small signals in his partners. Or perhaps it would not have been enjoyable with any other partner. Perhaps it was only Victoria and that indefinable quality that had reached out and grabbed him by the throat from the first moment he'd seen her.

He let the silence expand between them, let it settle over them like a cloak. Until he became exceedingly aware of the sound of her shallow breathing, of the sound of the elevator's gears grinding, moving them closer to their floor. To their destination.

It stopped, the door sliding open. Victoria's breath caught in her throat, her lips parted slightly, her eyes wide.

He reached out and touched the back of her neck, sliding his fingers around slowly, reveling in the velvet softness of her skin. He tightened his hold, guiding both of them from the elevator and out into the hall. She turned slightly, her eyes meeting his. There were questions there, but none that she spoke. And so he answered none of them. Instead, he kept his hold on her firm and continued down the corridor toward their suite.

He used the key card to unlock the door and held it open for her, waiting for her to enter. Another sign of her desire to be with him. And he needed another one. Because he had the feeling that once he touched her he would be at a point of no return, then he would find it almost impossible to stop were she to change her mind. So he had to be certain now.

He stood in the doorway and watched her walk to the center of the room, crimson against the white marble floor and the cream-colored furniture.

She dropped the wrap and the bag onto the sofa and looked up at him, biting her lower lip. It occurred to him then that he had not kissed her today. He had not kissed her since last night on the balcony, and he had not kissed her before that. Such a strange thing to want a woman as fiercely as he did when he had touched her so few times.

And suddenly he was desperate for more. Desperate to taste her deeper than he had before, longer.

He gripped the knot of his tie, loosening it as he crossed the room, closing the distance between them. And he watched as her tension began to dissolve, as she released a long slow breath, her shoulders lowering, her arms going to her sides. He could feel it reverberate inside of him, the release of her nerves, the embracing of desire. To be so in tune with a lover's body was an added dimension that he had not anticipated, nor one he had ever thought possible.

"Turn around, Victoria." He had an image in his mind of what it would look like to unzip the dress, and he was determined to see it brought to life.

She obeyed him, turning to face the back wall, her hands clasped in front of her.

He approached her slowly, placing his hand on her shoulder before trailing it down the center of her back to where to dress began, dipping his fingertip beneath the fabric. He leaned in, pressing a kiss to her shoulder blade, feeling her intake of breath as his lips made contact with her skin. He closed his eyes, kissed her again, lower this time. And lower still, until his mouth was at the line where fabric met flesh. He was on his knees before her, inhaling her scent, relishing her softness. He opened his eyes, looked at the contrast between the rich dark red of the gown and the pale white of her skin.

He took the tab of the zipper between his thumb and forefinger and began to draw it downward, exposing more of her body. He tugged it down past the border of her underwear, the same red as the dress, exposing her perfectly rounded ass for his inspection.

"I imagine," he said, his voice rough even to his own ears, "that you wear this style of underwear for practical reasons." He hooked his finger in the waistband of her panties, tracing the line where the fabric had just rested. "But I would like to think you wore them for me. I only wish I would've known that you had something so provocative on beneath the gown. There's no way I could've waited through that last hour."

Victoria said nothing in response, but no response was needed.

He pulled lightly on the dress and it fell, revealing her gorgeous body for his inspection. She was not wearing a bra; the style of dress she was wearing would never have allowed it. And now she was wearing nothing more than the extremely brief red panties. And a pair of black stilettos. It did things to him. Made him crave things. Everything.

He gripped her hips, turning her so that she was facing him, with him still on his knees. Leaving him at eye level with the most feminine part of her, barely concealed by the red lace of the G-string.

"And the shoes…you wore those for me, didn't you?"

She laughed, the sound shaky. "Not everything is all about you."

"Of course not." He kissed the tender skin of her stomach, just above the red lace, and felt her shiver beneath his touch. "Right now it's about you. I feel as though I might be working backward, seeing as I have not yet kissed your beautiful lips today."

And any moment now he would. But he was momentarily stunned by her beauty, and this position seemed the only one she was worthy of. One of reverence, one befitting the perfection that was before him now.

A fitting show of reverence before he took what he wanted.

Before he took what he needed.

He was still holding her hips, and he looked at the places where his skin covered hers. Tanned, calloused hands concealing her smoothness. Cheap tattoos he'd acquired on the streets a sharp contrast to the fine fabric that she normally kept pressed against her body. *Unworthy* was the only word that filled his mind now. He was not equal to the gift being offered.

But he would take it.

He would take it now.

He got to his feet, cupping her face and bringing her forward, bringing his mouth down hard on hers. She made a muffled sound, wrapping her arms around his neck and angling her head, parting her lips for him. He shifted, pulling her tightly to his body so that she was pressed against him completely, every inch of her touching every inch of him. He was still wearing the suit, layers of fabric between him and her beautiful near-naked body. It wasn't enough. It was nothing more than a tease. And he needed all of it, everything.

He suddenly felt desperate, as if he was drowning and she was air. As if he was sinking in quicksand and she was his lifeline.

The quaking feeling that had begun in the pit of his stomach in the ballroom intensified now. He closed his eyes tight, deepened the kiss, trying to get closer to her, in spite of the fact that there was no air at all between their bodies.

A jolt rocked him as her back came into contact with the wall. He had not realized that in his desperation for closeness he had moved them across the room. He had not realized because he wasn't aware of anything around them, wasn't aware of anything that expanded beyond the two of them. He wrenched his mouth away from hers and kissed her neck, down lower to her collarbone. She laced her fingers through his hair, holding him tightly to her. He kissed the valley between her breasts, tracing a line to her nipple with his tongue, relishing her flavor, her softness, her sweetness. He drew her deeply into his mouth, letting her hoarse cry wash over him, bathe him in satisfaction.

He straightened, kissing her lips again as he moved his hands over her curves, down to her hips, down lower until he got a grip on her thighs and tugged her legs up, hooking them around his waist so that he could carry her from the sitting area into his bedroom. She clung tightly to him, not releasing her hold until they arrived at the bed and he deposited her in the center of it.

He stepped back, looking at the picture she made, pale blond hair, pale skin over the white bedspread. The only color coming from the crimson thong that she still wore. It would have to go soon.

He shrugged his jacket off, letting it fall to the floor. Then he began to work the buttons on his shirt, wrenching the tie off completely and letting it go the way of the jacket. He made quick work of the shirt, then his belt, shoving his pants and underwear down to his ankles and kicking them to the side. And all the while he kept his eyes on Victoria, on her almost-dazed expression. There was a strange innocence in the way she looked at him, an innocence combined with a hunger that amped up his own.

"Your turn, Victoria." He wrapped his hand around his shaft, squeezing tightly as she lifted her hips and took hold of the side of her panties, drawing them down her legs, exposing the pale curls at the apex of her thighs.

He squeezed himself again, keeping his eyes fixed on her, the acute pleasure that rocked through him bordering on pain.

She lay there on the bed, on her back, propped up on her elbows, her breasts thrust into prominence, her thighs partly spread. She looked every inch the pure sacrifice, offered up to him. Waiting for him to consume her in fire.

A fitting analogy since she looked every bit like salvation, every bit like the deliverance he had always craved.

He shouldn't take her. But there were a lot of things in his life he'd done knowing he shouldn't.

He knelt on the foot of the bed and leaned forward, placing his hands on her stomach, sliding them down to her hips and pulling her forward so that the heart of her was only a breath away from his mouth. She reached out, taking hold of his shoulders. He looked up, met her gaze, saw fear and excitement in her eyes.

Keeping his eyes on hers, he lowered his head, drawing his tongue over her clitoris, watching as her expression changed, as her eyes fluttered closed, her head fell back. As she gave herself up to the experience. To him.

He turned his focus to tasting her, to pleasuring her as deeply as he could. Her flesh was slick beneath his tongue, sweet as honey. He pressed his finger to the entrance of her body, sliding it in slowly as he continued to tease and torture her with his mouth. She flexed her hips, pressing herself hard against him, drawing him in deeper.

He added a second finger, increasing the pressure and speed of his movements, until he felt her break. Her internal muscles pulsing around him, then a deep, throaty sound that had no restraint or decorum filling the room, signaling her release.

He withdrew from her body, kissing her hip bone, her stomach, her neck, settling himself between her thighs before kissing her deeply on the lips. "Yes, Victoria, yes. Give me everything. Give me your pleasure." He whispered the words against her lips, roughly, furtively.

She nodded, holding tightly to him, kissing his cheek, the corner of his mouth.

He said a brief prayer that the hotel staff had been thinking clearly, then reached for the nightstand. He breathed a sigh of relief when he found an unopened box of condoms. He made quick work of the wrapping and pulled out one of the packets, opening it quickly and sheathing himself before repositioning himself at the entrance of Victoria's body.

He began to slide inside of her, and she gasped as he did. She was tighter than he had anticipated, and he'd felt a slight resistance that he had never felt with previous lovers. He flexed his hips, driving into her to the hilt, and she dug her fingernails into his shoulders, her face screwed up tight.

"Victoria?"

Her eyes were still closed, her face turned to the side, her grip on his shoulders like iron. He said her name again and she shook her head, a signal, he assumed that she did not want him to speak. That she did not want to speak to him. He stayed frozen like that, until he couldn't bear it any longer.

He began to move inside of her, trying to keep his thrusts slow and measured, trying to find a way to bring her pleasure again, to ease the tension in her expression. He hadn't wanted to hurt her, he had not wanted…

Dear God, it wasn't possible that she'd been a virgin, was it?

And even as the thought filled him with horror, along with it came a sense of triumph that made him hate himself. And then, his mind was wiped clean, erased of any thought as pleasure overtook him.

She was slick, so wet for him, and after a few strokes she had her legs wrapped around his hips, sweet sounds of pleasure escaping her lips. She arched against him with each thrust, and he ground his pelvis against the source of her pleasure, focusing himself on bringing her to completion again. He gritted his teeth, trying to hold on to his control. And when he felt her come again he released his hold.

He reached around and cupped her butt, pulling her hard up against him, his movements erratic, strong, no finesse present at all. There was only this. Only Victoria. Only the tight, wet heat of her body and the blinding pleasure that was building inside of him, so big, so strong, he was sure that it would break him.

And then it broke, and on a roar he found his own climax, release raging through him like an inferno. Devastating everything in its path, leaving the ground scorched and clear, cleansed.

When he returned to himself, he was breathing hard; his head rested against Victoria's neck, his entire body shaking.

And his brain started to piece together everything that had happened. And what it meant.

He moved away from her, the shaking feeling that had started hours ago worse now. He stood at the foot of the bed, looking at her, trying to figure out what she was thinking.

She shifted slightly and he saw a dark spot of red staining the formerly pristine bedspread. An accusation that screamed louder than words ever could have.

"Why didn't you tell me?" he asked.

He felt dizzy, sick. Because, dimly, he realized that he had known all along. That he had been drawn to her for almost this very reason. Because he was a sick bastard who had been desperate for her innocence. To use her as atonement, as if she could cleanse him. As if she could erase the past.

The sacrificial lamb complete with an offering of blood.

As if it could ever erase his past. As if he could trade this blood for the blood he had spilled so long ago. As if somehow being with her would restore what he had lost.

Instead, he saw himself clearly. Saw this clearly for what it was.

He knew what it was like to have his innocence ripped away. And he knew what it was to have the person you had sacrificed for turn you away after.

But she had a choice. She made a choice.

She hadn't known, though. Not really.

He would hurt her. He couldn't keep her. Because after this was over he would send her away, benefiting greatly from what she had done for him, claiming it for his own and giving her nothing in return.

He felt sick. He felt as if he needed air.

Without saying a word he turned away from her and walked out of the room. He threw open the double doors that led out to the balcony and walked outside naked, letting the heavy, sultry air settle over his bare skin.

He had thought to use her as a means of salvation. Had excused it all because she'd given her permission. Because she'd made a choice, and that was what truly mattered.

But he saw now that this was just more blood he had spilled.

Blood he would never be able to wash off no matter how hard he tried.

CHAPTER TEN

VICTORIA WASN'T ENTIRELY certain if she was breathing or not. She was sure that she couldn't move. She was still lying on her back, naked, the cold air harsh against her bare breasts, her skin still slick with sweat. His, and hers.

The intimacy of it all rocked her, sent a shiver through her even now. He had been inside of her, closer to her than any other person had ever been in her entire life. The pleasure, though it had been mind-blowing, was almost beside the point. For the first time in so many years, more years than she could count, she had felt connected to another person. Really connected. Not just operating around them, trying to move the pieces of her life into the proper positioning to gain acceptance. To look as if she was doing well.

They had been the kind of close where you couldn't fake anything. Because she had shaken while he held her in his arms, and he had trembled above her. Because she had felt him pulse inside of her as he had given himself up to his orgasm, and her internal muscles had clinched tight around him as she had found her own.

There had been no control, nothing but honesty.

And then he had seen that little spot of blood on the bedspread and gone tearing from the room.

She supposed she should have been honest with him. But then, it hadn't seemed that it would be relevant. It wasn't as if they lived in Regency England. Her hymen was her business. Anyway, she hadn't actually imagined she would have one at this point. Apparently she had.

She took in a deep breath and rolled out of the bed, her thigh muscles shaking. She felt dizzy and disoriented, but she had to go and find her lover.

Her *lover*. There was something about that. Something wonderful and terrifying all at the same time.

Which sort of summed up her first time, now she thought about it.

Being in his arms had been wonderful, having him leave, less so.

She walked out of the bedroom and noticed that the doors to the balcony were open and she headed straight for them, not caring that she wasn't wearing any clothes. The warm air wrapped itself around her skin like a lush robe, banishing the chill brought on by the air-conditioning and Dmitri's absence.

She looked around and saw him on the far end of the balcony, as though he was trying to blend into the inky blackness that surrounded them.

"You'll have to forgive me," she said, starting to walk toward him, "I am a novice at all of this, so I'm not quite sure how things work yet. Is it customary to play post-coital hide-and-seek?"

"You might have said something. About your novice status."

She lifted a shoulder. "I said I was inexperienced."

"Inexperienced is not entirely absent experience."

She let out a loud, exasperated breath. "No, I suppose not. But then, you were the one who made assumptions. Based on what I told you about Nathan, I imagine. And I didn't really want to clear them up because it's all sort of embarrassing."

"How is it he didn't have you?" he asked, his voice rough.

She cleared her throat. "Not for lack of me offering. I met him in my bedroom one evening when he came to see me. Totally naked. And he looked at me, wrapped me in a blanket and told me things couldn't be like that. He looked at me like I was so sad. So delusional." She shook her head. "I felt stupid. Rejected. And when I found out he was after my father's company? It was even worse. Not that I wished I'd slept with someone who was tricking me, but…but he was a villain. And even then he didn't want to take advantage of me. He just wanted to manipulate me."

"There is nothing wrong with you, Victoria," he said, his voice rough.

"Maybe not. But he made me doubt my body, my heart, my brains…everything. And then on top of that he cost me my relationship with my dad. I have wanted nothing more than to fix things with my father. But I'm starting to think that I never will. Not really. Even if he gets London Diva back I'm not sure that he'll ever look at me the way I wish he would. And I wonder why I care. So tonight I didn't. I did this for me. I probably should've said something to you, but…I didn't want to take the chance that you would reject me. This was the first time in a long time I wanted something for me, and only me. I didn't want to lose that." She took a deep, shaking breath. "I was afraid you wouldn't like it. I was afraid I would do something wrong. Apparently I did."

This rejection hurt worse than any other that came before it. Probably because she had given so much. Because she had made herself so vulnerable, when she hated to do that. It made her question herself again, and she'd never wanted to be in that position again. It was why she'd avoided this kind of relationship, why she'd avoided men.

Why she'd wrapped herself in armor so thick no one could reach her.

But she'd let him reach her, and it already hurt.

He laughed, a frightening, hollow sound. "You think I did not like it?" He began to walk toward her, out of the shadow. "You do not understand. The problem is that I liked it far too much. Do you have any idea how hard it makes me to realize that I'm the only man to ever be inside of you? That I'm the first man you've ever been with? Do you know what it does to me? Do you know how it turns me on to realize that I took your innocence?"

"No, no I don't." Her heart was pounding hard, her blood roaring through her ears.

"It does. Because I wanted that. I needed it. Do you realize how sick that is? Do you realize how little right I have to that? I am…" He looked around them, as though he might find the answers to the end of his sentence somewhere in the air. "I am the last man on earth who should have ever been allowed to touch you. I used you. Because if there's one thing a jaded, damaged, sinful soul desires it's the taste of something innocent. And I would consume it. Take it all until you have nothing left. Because there will never be enough to take away this feeling inside of me. To make me feel new. I'm damaged beyond fixing and it was unfair of me to try to use you to put a bandage on it. There are some wounds that don't heal, and the wounds on my soul are among them."

His words hit her hard, strange. As if she was reaching in the dark to try to find some understanding and coming up empty. "I don't understand what you mean, Dmitri. If you think that somehow you being a fighter makes you unworthy of me, you could not be further from the truth. I've made mistakes—I might have been a virgin but I'm far from innocent. I understand the way that life is. I understand the way that people are."

He advanced on her, placing his hand on her cheek, sliding his thumb across her cheekbone. "Oh, Victoria, you have been betrayed, and I don't doubt that. I do not seek to minimize it. But you are innocent. You know nothing of the evil in the world, and I would hate to be the reason that you learned about it."

"So you're just going to profess to using me and leave it at that? That doesn't work. It doesn't work for me."

"I don't want to compound my sins."

"I don't want to be your damned vestal virgin. Stop ascribing something to me that I don't deserve. I've hardly been wafting around the planet wearing flowing white robes for the past twenty-eight years, untouched by both men and nature. I've lived life. I've been a part of life. The charities I'm a part of mean that I hear terrible stories. About starving children, about disease, about abuse. My eyes are open, trust me. You gave me a choice. I made it. It's not yours to regret."

"Do you know why I'm so angry at myself for what I've done to you?"

"Enlighten me, Dmitri, because I have a feeling if I start trying to guess I'm only going to make myself angrier."

"I know what it's like to have your innocence stolen from you. And to have the gift rejected."

"I don't... I'm not sure I understand."

"I'm not talking about sex. But it's far too close to the scenario for my liking."

"Stop being vague. This is hardly the place for it. I am standing out here on a balcony, naked with you. I have just had sex for the first time in my life. The fact I waited for so long should tell you what a big deal this is for me. I'm naked," she said again, "in more ways than one. Perhaps you could offer me a little bit of honesty?"

"You do not want to have this discussion with me, Victoria."

She took a step toward him. "Stop telling me what I want, Dmitri."

"You know that I'm a fighter, but what would you say if you knew I was a killer?"

His words poured over her, and it felt strange. As though someone had doused her in warm water, the trickle of heat fuzzy, numbing at first, until it faded out into a prickling cold. "I don't...I don't understand."

"Of course you don't. Because it's too difficult for you to believe. Because for all that you seem to think you are cynical, I don't believe you really are. You still want to think the best of me. I know you do. I can see you attempted to justify what I'm about to say already."

"What happened?"

"I was not born on the streets of Moscow. I am the son of a high-ranking official in the Russian army. At one time in his life my father was a good man. But he was a part of some sort of tactical operation that changed him. All I know is that people around him were killed, his friends, his comrades. I know he felt a lot of guilt. I know he was never the same after. He was depressed at first, sad. He drank a lot. And at some point he began taking it all out on my mother. The violence increased. Over the years I became terrified of him, terrified for her, and for myself. One day I came home from school and he was standing there, my mother in the corner, and he was holding two guns."

"Dmitri..." She found she did want to stop him from talking, did want to stop him from telling the story. Because she knew this was the sort of thing that she would never be able to escape once it was in her mind. Once she knew what happened next she could never go back to un-knowing it. And yet, he had lived through it. And she had shared her body with him. She had to let him share this.

"He asked me if I wanted to play a game. He said we would play chicken. We would see who would lose their nerve first. And he tossed me the gun. He raised his gun and pointed it at my mother. And I proved to him in that last moment that there were lines I would not allow to be crossed. It is a pity I don't think he was ever conscious of that. Because I don't think he ever knew what hit him. I don't think he had another thought after that. Because I pulled the trigger and I ended him."

"He deserved it," she said. The words came out without her permission, with every ounce of conviction in her body. "You can't possibly feel guilty."

"I don't," he said, the words hard, rough. "But the fact remains that when you take a life it changes you. When you see someone's soul leave their body, when you watch their life bleed out of them onto expensive wooden floors, it changes who you are. You lose a part of yourself. I'm not a terribly religious man, but sometimes I think a part of my soul went with his. That some piece of me is burning down there along with him."

She swallowed hard, her hands shaking, her entire body shaking. "That isn't true."

"I don't think you're qualified to decide that."

And she knew she wasn't.

"What happened after that?"

"The military stepped in. Internally, they did an inquiry and called it self-defense, but saw no point in publicizing it. They did not want to bring any negative press against the government, did not want any light shone on the mission my father had been involved in that caused his trauma. So they swept it under the rug."

"What happened next?"

"My mother threw me out of my home. She said she did not want me there. Not after what I had done. She called me a killer and worse. And it didn't matter that I knew I had had no other choice. The end result was the same. I gave up a part of myself, a part of who I had been for her. And she sent me away. All of it...every bit of it was out of my control. I had no choice."

Suddenly, the leather cuff made sense. His dedication to giving her a choice. And his words about taking from her...

"You didn't take a part of me, Dmitri. You gave something back."

She let the words hang between them. They were quickly consumed by the sound of revelers below, by a distant sound of music, different songs weaving together. And yet, her words still seemed to remain prominent. Looming large, impossible to ignore.

He needed to know. He needed to understand.

"Victoria, I can't have..."

She closed the distance, her heart thundering rapidly, and wrapped her arms around him, pulling him close to her. "I don't care. I don't care what you've done. Because what you've done for me is more important." She didn't know if she'd said the right words. They were inadequate; they weren't deep, or meaningful. But they were all she could say. Everything else was jumbled up inside of her, caught up in a churning current of need so that she could scarcely hear her own thoughts.

"Take me back inside," she continued. "Take me back inside and make love to me again."

"You can't want me to touch you. Not now. Not knowing what you do."

She extricated herself from his hold and wrapped her hands around his wrist, bringing his palm into contact with her breast, pressing his hand firmly against her flesh. "I want you to touch me. I want you to touch me like only you have ever done. If what happened back there was you taking my innocence, then finish the job. Take it all. Take it all for yourself. Change me completely. Make me yours."

"All I will ever do is take from you. I can't give you anything."

"That's where you're wrong. You've already given me something. You've already given me everything."

"I took your virginity. That was all for me."

"No. You gave me passion."

He stared at her, dark eyes glittering in the dim light. "I should turn away from you. But I can't. I think it's that damned, missing part of my soul."

"If it's the thing that allows you to be with me, then I hope you never find it."

"Well, as I think it's already burning in hell, I might as well go ahead and secure the trip for the rest of me."

She cupped his face, keeping her eyes fixed on his. "Neither of us has to worry about hell tonight. Because when I'm with you I feel like you've taken me to heaven."

"Being with you is likely the only chance I'll ever have to experience that." He bent and kissed her, the context desperate, intense. When they parted, they were both breathing hard. "I cannot give you any more than this."

"I understand."

"When our arrangement is over, this will be over, too. You can be my lover in New York, and through the event in London. But once the ownership of your father's boutiques is returned to your family, this will end."

"Of course." The thought of it made her ache, made her feel as if her heart was bleeding. She didn't want to say goodbye to him. She already knew that. And yet, she also knew there was no place in her life for an ex-MMA fighter with blood on his hands. With tattoos on his skin, with no conscience to speak of.

She knew he wouldn't fit into her old life. And she tried to ignore the deep, yawning ache inside of her that told her she didn't want to go back to her old life anyway.

"But until then, I will have you. As often as I like. However I like."

A shiver wound through her, a burning excitement that she had never experienced before. "I'm yours."

And she meant it.

But she knew that no matter whether it made sense or not, she meant it beyond New York. She meant it to be on the final event in London, beyond the moment London Diva would be returned to her family.

In that moment, she realized that no matter whether it made sense or not, she was Dmitri Markin's forever.

And in that same moment she realized that he would never be hers.

It was enough that it should make her turn away from him. That it should make her stop everything that was happening now.

But instead she kissed him again. Kissed him again knowing that all of this would end in heartbreak.

It would be worth it.

Because for the first time since she was sixteen years old, she felt alive. And even though she knew it would end in nothing but pain, she would embrace it. Because if she couldn't have them forever, she would have him now. She would have him for as long as was possible.

Until the bitter end.

CHAPTER ELEVEN

"WELL, I THINK that went rather well, don't you, Mr. Charity Director?"

Victoria looked across the hotel room at Dmitri, who was standing by the bed, still wearing his suit from tonight's charity event. It had been nearly a week since they'd left New Orleans and started preparations for what had been a smashing success here in New York.

All headlines seemed to indicate that approval for Dmitri's efforts were on the rise, and more importantly, the amount of money that had been pledged so far indicated that, as well.

"It's very hard for me to tell. I had to wear a suit and make inane conversation. Also I had to get up in front of a crowd and make a speech. None of that reads as good to me. But you might be a better judge than I."

"These are the hazards of being in the public eye, Dmitri." She looked at him, at his handsome face, his lean figure outlined to perfection by the suit. Her heart started beating faster. As it always did when she was near him. And rather than getting better since they became lovers, it had only got more intense. So maybe that was better. Depending on what scale you were using to measure. Of course, things intensifying between them as time progressed wasn't ideal, seeing as days passing meant the countdown timer on the relationship was winding down.

"It went well. The media is already calling you a massive success. New Orleans was perfect, and I'm sure the headline for tonight's event will be just as glittering." She was determined not to think too much about the end of things, or her feelings.

"Then I trust you."

"I'm not completely certain you do, but I'll take it."

"I trust you as much as I trust anyone, Victoria." He reached up and began loosening the knot on his tie.

"Really?"

"Yes. Of course, that isn't saying much. I don't trust anyone."

"Well, that does undermine the compliment."

She watched him standing there, his hands held awkwardly at his sides, as though he was at loose ends. As though he wasn't certain what to do. That wasn't typical. Dmitri was a fighter, and she could usually see it in every line of his body. There was always a readiness to his stance, as though he was prepared to engage a mortal enemy at a moment's notice. But just now he looked as if he was contemplating running. And that was not like the Dmitri she knew it all.

"It does not. If anything, it should let you know how rare this sort of relationship is for me."

"Sexual relationships?" she asked.

"Intimacy," he said. "We have been staying together. Sleeping together. That is an expression of trust. You might cut my throat while I dream, after all."

"I wouldn't," she said, her own throat tightening.

"I know," he said. "I trust that. Victoria, when you live as I have, you learn to keep control. To keep all of your power and give nothing to anyone else. Because people will take your life and reroute it as they see fit. Steal all the money you earned in a fight, rob you of your bed for the night. I learned early on to make sure I controlled my surroundings. But you…you test me, my sweet. I find I lose my control. My focus."

Such raw, honest words from her lover, an admission she knew cost him. One that burned through her, made her want to accept his gift and hold it close. And test it at the same time.

"If I take off my dress will I regain some of your focus?" His dark eyes met with hers, and she relished the intensity in them. All for her.

"It wouldn't hurt."

She reached out and pushed one strap down her shoulder, keeping her eyes fixed on his. "So, are you in the mood to talk?"

He undid a cuff on his dress shirt, his dark eyes locked on hers. "Why would I ever be in the mood to talk when I could bury myself in your beautiful body instead?"

His words sent a shock of sensation through her. Only a week ago, it would have embarrassed her, had her muscles tightening up. Now his words, the intent in his eyes, made her feel on fire. Alive. Made her want to push back. To take possession of him as he'd done to her. "Darling, the question is why would I ever be in the mood to talk when I could have you inside of me?"

Her words were bold, and for a second she was shocked by herself. But in a good way. She had always been confident in her own business, in the work she did for various charities. But when it came to her feelings, her desires, she always felt the need to push them down tight, shut the lid on them and lock them up. She had never felt free to express them, not after the mistake she made. Because she had been convinced that there was something fundamentally wrong with them, with her.

She'd been terrified of exposing her vulnerabilities to

anyone, even to herself. Of risking rejection again. Telling a man that she wanted him to be inside of her was definitely putting her at risk of exposing her vulnerabilities. Of letting him know that he was her vulnerability.

But she didn't care, and she didn't feel weak. She felt empowered. She felt more comfortable in her own body, in her own skin than ever before.

Those old memories, those old rejections, were washed away by the desire in Dmitri's eyes.

He stared her down, lifting his chin slightly. As though she were an opponent in the ring, and he saw the challenge being issued. Accepted it. Welcomed it.

She knew beyond a shadow of a doubt that he wanted her, could tell by the gleam in his dark eyes, by the tension in every line of his body. More than that, she was confident in the fact that she wanted him, and that it was okay. In this moment, she had no doubts, not in him, not in herself.

She pushed the other strap of her dress down, taking a deep breath and allowing herself to be conscious of the way that her breasts rose above the neckline of the fabric, the red silk just concealing her nipples, exposing the rest. She'd worn red again, because she knew he liked it. And then she looked at him again, at his awareness. And it increased her own. The way he watched her, the intensity with which he kept his eyes trained on her, heightening her arousal, her confidence.

Such a strange thing, because only a few days ago she could never have done this. Could never have stood in front of the man and taken her dress off. She would have felt that she was too much in danger of losing control, and the simple fact was that she had lost control. But Dmitri was losing it with her, and that equality made it feel, if not safe, then at least as if she wasn't alone.

As long as she could cling to him it didn't matter. It

didn't matter if she was in control, because she was holding on to him. He was a fighter; he was strong. And so was she.

She reached behind herself and gripped the tab of her zipper, drawing it down slowly, letting it fall down around her waist. Again, she wasn't wearing a bra underneath, the lining of the dress providing all the structure she needed for her modest curves. She was rewarded by the sharp sound of a breath hissing through his teeth, by the pitch of his muscular chest as everything in him froze while he took in the sight of her.

In response, her heart began beating faster, the pulse at the base of her throat throbbing. An answering pulse beating at the apex of her thighs. She knew what this was now, knew what she wanted. And she knew that she could only get it from him. Because it was about more than sex, it was about the connection.

He had played off the trust that he felt toward her, but she did trust him. She trusted that he would do what he said, that he was a man of his word. She trusted that when she fell he would catch her. And outside of this relationship, this moment, this room, she didn't know what would happen. But here and now, she knew she could trust him. With her body, if not her heart.

Though, she had given him her heart nonetheless.

The thought made her feel more naked than revealing skin ever could have.

She pushed the dress down her hips, taking her underwear with it, letting them fall to the floor. The pool of crimson at her feet, like blood, spilled just for him. Her soul, bleeding out, hemorrhaging. And only he could stop it. Just as she would only allow such a thing for him.

He sat down on the edge of the bed, his eyes never leaving her body. He reached up and loosened the knot on his tie, but touched nothing else. He rested his hands on either side of his thighs, his legs spread just a bit, giving her a view of his hardening arousal.

She walked toward him, black high heels still on her feet, the soles of the shoes clicking on the white marble floor. He'd bought the stilettos for her in New Orleans, and he'd proceeded to bend her over the couch the night they'd brought them back to the hotel.

They were the kind of shoes they'd spoken about before. The kind she knew he liked. And she would use them to her advantage.

She was completely naked except for those shoes, and she felt no shame. She felt no embarrassment. She wanted to show him. Wanted to take the spark she saw in his eyes and turn it into an inferno. Use her curves as the fuel for that fire. This confidence, this desire came from inside of her, but he was the one who had unlocked it. And so it was for him, in this moment, it was all for him.

She approached the bed, standing between his legs, placing her forefinger beneath his chin and tilting his face upward. "You did well." She wanted him to understand that, wanted him to realize all of the things he had to offer. Wanted him to fully take on board the fact that he was doing good, that he was changing lives. Using his success to affect the destiny of others.

He lifted his hand, curling his fingers around the back of her thigh, drawing her closer to him, bringing the most intimate part of her so close to his mouth it made her ache. He leaned in, kissing her stomach, sending a quiver of need straight to her core.

He let his hand drift up slowly, squeezing her but gently, sliding his palm over the sensitive skin. "You are beautiful. You know that, don't you, Victoria?"

She had never worried much about her looks. She dressed and applied makeup to give the best impression possible, and she had always been relatively happy with the results. But Dmitri made her feel *beautiful*. Not just pleased with her appearance, but he gave her the feeling that she radiated something only he could see. Something that he appreciated to the depth of his soul in a way no one else ever had.

"More importantly," she said, "I know that I'm beautiful to you."

It was a clumsy way to express what she felt, but it was all she had.

He kissed her stomach again, lowering his head slightly, tracing a line with the tip of his tongue from her belly button to just above the place that was wet and aching for him. He looked up at her, his eyes locked with hers. Some might consider him to be sitting in the submissive position at the moment, but Victoria knew that he was the one who owned this moment. Who held her in thrall. Desperate for what he might do next, unable to do anything but stand, shaking, ready, waiting.

"And am I beautiful to you, my sweet Victoria?" His question stopped her cold, made her heart stutter in her chest.

More evidence of him opening himself to her. Giving her control.

She reached down and cupped his cheek, keeping her eyes on his. "My entire life has been surrounded by beauty. By fine things, lovely houses. Museums, parties. Man-made things that have been polished until they shone. Until they have had every spot and blemish removed from them. But you, Dmitri, are a wild thing. A beast who seems to have pulled me into his lair. You are not perfect. You are scarred." She traced the crooked line of his nose, down to the fine scar that bisected his upper lip. "Marked permanently by the places you've been, by the pain you have suffered." She moved her fingertips down to his muscular forearm, traced the dark marks of ink that stained his skin. "And yet I find you are perfectly beautiful to me. You make me see for the first time the beauty in imperfection." *The beauty in my own imperfection.* She left the last part unspoken. Held it close to her chest, close to her heart.

She didn't need him to be perfect, and suddenly it occurred to her that maybe she didn't need to be perfect, either. That maybe she shouldn't need to be perfect to be loved. After all, she loved Dmitri and he was the furthest thing from perfect she could imagine. But he was perfect for her. Necessary in a way she never would have thought possible.

He had changed her, in every way that mattered. Changed the way she felt and thought about herself and the world.

He said nothing. Instead, he pulled her forward so that one knee was resting on the bed, bringing the heart of her into line with his mouth. He leaned forward, sliding his tongue along her damp flesh, skimming the bundle of nerves that was aching for his touch. Sending a white-hot bolt of pleasure through her, leaving her shaken, leaving her burned.

He growled, holding on to her with both hands, bringing her hard up against his mouth, his exploration of her ruthless, demanding. She gasped, holding herself steady by clinging to his shoulders, knowing that if she let go she would find herself melted into a puddle on the floor, or perhaps drifting away from the earth entirely. She wasn't certain which. But then, she wasn't certain where the floor was, or where the ceiling was. She wasn't certain if they were even in the hotel room anymore at all.

Because there was nothing but this, nothing but Dmitri, nothing but his touch. His perfect, altering touch.

He adjusted his hold on her, placing one hand between her thighs, teasing her slick entrance with his fingertip as he continued to tease her with his tongue.

Pleasure twisted in her stomach, nice, sharp and unyielding, pressing deeper and deeper until she was certain she couldn't take it anymore. Until she was certain she couldn't withstand it. A harsh sound escaped her lips, and he pressed his finger deep inside of her, timing the thrusts with the strokes of his tongue. Pleasure broke over her like warm oil coating her skin, waves of deep pleasure echoing through her.

On shaking legs she stood, moving away from the bed and walking to the nightstand that was beside it. They had both ensured that condoms were in the drawer upon arrival. Because condoms held top spot on Victoria's brand-new priorities list. She procured a plastic packet as quickly as possible and tore it open, setting it on the mattress so that she could make quick use of it later. Among the new skills she had acquired since meeting Dmitri, speedy contraceptive application was one of them.

"Stand up. And take off your clothes," she said, her tone crisp.

A wicked smile curved Dmitri's lips. "Anything to please you," he said, his voice a rough purr that reverberated through her body.

"Do I have control?" she asked, her voice trembling. "Will you give this to me?"

"You might have to take it," he said, his tone like iron, a core of challenge moving through his words.

"Surrender doesn't mean as much when it's taken," she said, unsure of where the words had come from.

"You think not?" he asked.

But he stood and began slowly and methodically removing the pieces of his suit. Sliding his tie through the shirt collar, letting his black jacket drop to the floor. He unbuckled his belt, let it hang open as he set about undoing the buttons on his shirt.

Yet again the power balance shifted. She might be the one giving commands, but everything inside of her went weak watching Dmitri expose his body to her. She was a captive audience as he removed his shirt, as the muscles and lines in his body shifted and bunched. And then he pushed his pants down, exposing his muscular thighs. Not to mention the most male part of him. Thick, proud, a statement of just how much he wanted her.

"Lie down on the bed." Her voice was trembling now, and she thought to keep the authority in her tone.

"Aren't you going to say please, Victoria?" he asked, the darkness in his eyes lit by a black flame.

She steeled herself, lifted her chin, her eyes never leaving his. "No. I won't say please, Dmitri. Now lie back on the bed, or I'll walk out of the room and leave you there like that, hard and aching for me. Is that what you want?"

"So I don't have a choice?" he asked, his voice set with stone.

She swallowed hard. "You have a choice," she said, knowing this was the most important thing for him to hear. "With me, you always have a choice."

"But you will leave if I do not comply."

She nodded slowly. "Not all choices are good." Something was happening, something big, a war raging in the empty spaces between them. A fight, not for bodies, but for souls. "Say it."

He wrapped his hand around his erection, squeezed tight. "I don't want you to leave me like this, Victoria. I need you." He moved his palm over his length. "I could do this myself, but it wouldn't be the same. It has to be you."

He was giving this to her. And it made her want to push. Want to take even more than he was offering.

Her heart was hammering hard, need making her shake. "Good."

He sat back down on the edge of the mattress, then slid backward, positioning himself at the center of the bed, lying on his back. "Now what?"

He was turning over all of the control, and the action made her heart feel as if it was being squeezed. "Put your hands above your head."

His eyes still locked with hers, he obeyed her command. The action stretched his ab muscles, allowed her to see the definition in his torso to an even greater degree. Suddenly, an image burned itself into her brain, one she hadn't expected, a fantasy she'd never had before. But she wanted it now. Wanted to see how far she could push this. How far she could push his trust in her.

I trust you as much as I trust anyone.

He'd said it, but unless she tested it…how would she know?

She had to know.

She bent down and picked up the black silk tie from the floor. She ran her fingers over the cool fabric, stretching it tight between her hands. "The first day that I saw you, you were fighting. You're so strong, Dmitri. The strongest man I have ever known. But I want to make you mine." She walked closer to the bed, lifted her leg and pressed her knee into the mattress. "Do you trust me?"

"With my life."

And it was everything she had ever needed, a balm for her soul she hadn't realized would heal the cracks and scars that had been placed there by that long-ago indiscretion. By the reaction her family had had to it.

Dmitri trusted her. After years of not even trusting herself, it felt like a miracle.

"Give me this," she said.

"Here? In this way?" he asked, his words splintered. "I will give you anything you desire."

He stayed in the exact position she had commanded him to assume, watching her. She had the feeling he was like a predator, hiding his strength, hiding his intent, in the stillness of his muscles. But that at any moment he could spring forward and capture her. That was what gave the moment so much power. He could physically overpower her; there was no question about that. The only control that she had was given to her by him. It was a gift, and she was determined to use it wisely. To use it well.

She positioned herself so that she was all the way on the bed, keeping the tie gripped firmly in her hand as she stretched over his body, dropping a light kiss on his lips. He remained motionless, as though he was carved from stone. She lifted his hands, still pressed together above his head. She traced the inside of his wrist with her fingertips, the blue veins that were visible there, the dark slashing lines of the tattoo. The cuff she'd given him the first night she'd decided to give herself to him. When she'd made the choice to have him.

How far she had come. How far they had come.

She laid the tie flat across his skin, watching for his reaction. Heat flared deep in his eyes, but his face remained immovable. His lips were pressed into a firm line; he clenched his jaw tight. Arousal, she recognized it. He wanted this. She could see it clearly.

She curved the two ends of the tie around behind his hands, before crossing them and bringing them around to the front, knotting them tight. Then she placed her hands over his, pressing them deep into the pillows, as she leaned down and kissed his lips.

This, she recognized as the ultimate surrender. Not his, but hers. Surrendering to the deep desire that clawed at her insides, to a need that transcended social acceptability, that transcended what was right, what she should want, what she should do. This was a surrender to the desire that Dmitri made her feel.

And he was accepting it, reveling in it, not making her feel as if there was anything wrong with her, but on the contrary, making her feel as if her desires were a beautiful thing. Something he wanted, something he craved.

She reached for the condom that she had left sitting on the edge of the mattress and pulled the thin sheath from the packet, wrapping her hand around his arousal and sliding it on quickly. His body arched upward, his expression pained now. She straddled him, her heat lining up with his erection.

"Victoria." His voice was rough, reflecting the look on his face.

"Impatient?" She was the one who felt impatient, hollow, aching.

He growled, rolling his hips beneath her, his hardness sliding against the slickness between her thighs. She was reasonably certain that if he wanted to he could break the restraints, or at the very least he could move his arms so that they were around her, so that the power balance was shifted. But he did not. He steadfastly obeyed the order she had given him. Honored the unspoken agreement that had passed between them.

"Are you impatient, Dmitri?" She repeated the question. And he remained silent. "Answer me, or I will leave."

He had to say it, he had to tell her that he wanted this as badly as she did. He had to let her know that he was a slave to it as much as she was. That he wasn't just captive in body, but in spirit. That this man, this fighter, was surrendering himself to her.

He had told her, over and over, that the power was his. It was something he prized, and he had made that clear. Yet here he was, handing her the power. Handing her the control.

And at every step, she would make him choose to give it. A conscious surrender.

"I am impatient," he said, clenching his teeth.

"What do you want?"

"I want to be inside you. More than I want my next breath."

She shifted their position, flexing her hips, bringing the blunt, thick head of him to the entrance of her body. She teased them both, lowering herself slowly onto his hardened length, relishing the slow satisfaction of being filled by him, inch by excruciating inch. And she watched his face, watched the tendons in his neck standing out, his jaw tight, a muscle twitching there from the restraint it took for him to remain as he was.

"Victoria, I can—" What followed was a long string of Russian, the words a mystery to her, but the tone clear.

So she gave him what he wanted, what they both wanted. She moved over him, slowly at first, establishing a rhythm that built the tension between them. She braced her hands on either side of him, keeping her eyes on the black fabric over his wrists, watching as he tightened his hands into fists.

She shifted, straightening, riding him harder, planting her hand at the center of his chest, feeling his heart raging against her palm. His skin was slick with sweat, his skin was hot. She moved against him, rocking her clitoris against him, bringing herself closer to the peak. And she could feel him drawing closer, too. She felt responsible for it in this position, more responsible for his needs than ever before.

She leaned down, pressing her body flush against his, pressing her breasts against his chest, kissing him deeply, as she flexed her hips one last time, pushing them both over the edge. She could feel him pulsing inside of her, her internal muscles squeezing him tight as they both rode out the storm. When it was over she lay there, her head resting against his chest, listening to the steady beat of his heart. Listening as it slowed, as his breathing became even again.

And for a moment, she simply stayed there and held tightly to him, terrified by the sudden realization that she couldn't keep him here. Not if she bound his hands, not if she clung to him.

Tonight he had surrendered to her, tonight he had chosen her. But tomorrow would be different.

At the end of all this, he would walk away. And there were no restraints in her possession that would keep him with her.

CHAPTER TWELVE

DMITRI FOUGHT HARD to catch his breath, but he found he could not. Feelings were prowling through his chest like beasts, tearing everything they could wrap their jaws around. And still, this silk was tied around his wrists. And he wasn't hurrying to break the bonds. There was something intoxicating about it. About allowing her to hold him captive. About being possessed by her.

It touched something deep inside of him, the boy that he had been then, the boy who had been thrown out of his home in Moscow after sacrificing his entire soul to free his mother from a monster. After having his sacrifice rejected.

It wasn't a sacrifice, there was no choice.

But Victoria had given him a choice. And Victoria had made her choices.

Victoria had done something entirely different. Victoria had made it clear that she wanted him here, that she wanted him with her. The ties around his wrists spoke louder than any words, and her arms around his waist, her head resting on his chest, spoke louder still.

She shifted, kissing his chest, the light pressure hitting him with the force of an opponent's blow. This had felt like a fight, and in the end he wanted to surrender.

To her, to being hers.

He had never thought about it before in quite those terms, but the fact remained that most people in life belonged to someone else. Either to their parents, to their spouse, or to a friend. Dmitri could not remember the last time he had ever belonged to anyone. Certainly his mentor had been a driving force in his life, but their relationship had not extended outside the ring. His father had gone crazy, and in the end Dmitri had been the one to remove him from this world. And his mother had detached from him so easily it was clear he had never truly belonged to her.

But Victoria... She was different. This was different.

And it was terrifying. It made him feel as if he was at a crossroads yet again, wrenched open and exposed.

It was the hidden cost of giving her his control. It gave her a way in. Past his defenses. And he had sworn to himself he would never do that again.

He tugged against his restraints, against her, suddenly unable to breathe. "Untie me," he said, his tone hard.

Victoria scrambled to free him, shaking fingers fumbling as she removed the tie from around his wrists. He probably could've done it himself. But he needed her to do it. It had to be her choice.

He sat up and rubbed his wrists, even though they didn't hurt. The bonds had been gentle, but the impression of them lingered. And he wanted them gone.

"This game is done," he said, swinging his legs over the side of the bed and moving into a standing position.

He didn't know what he had expected her to do, but he had not expected her expression to morph into one of pure steel. Her lips flattened into a straight line, her eyes glittering with determination. "Why? Because it scares you? Because you're afraid of me?"

"I'm not afraid of you, princess. If I were afraid of you I wouldn't have let you tie my hands." But he was afraid. Because he was on the verge of something he'd avoided for years. A turning point he either had to accept, or run from.

"Oh, that? Am I supposed to be impressed by the fact that you allowed me to tie you up when we both know you could've fought me off if you truly wanted to?"

Rage poured through him, and he couldn't fathom quite why what she'd said made him so angry. "Do not minimize it. You have no idea what that cost me. I surrendered my control to you. And the last time I allowed someone else to force my hand I pulled the trigger of a gun and ended a man's life, so do not minimize what I have given," he repeated.

"Dmitri…"

"Do you know where I got the leather cuff?" he asked.

"What…the one you gave me? You said it was nothing."

"I am a liar, Victoria. You should not be surprised to learn that."

"Where, then?" she asked, her voice muted.

"Off my father's dead body," he said, his words falling flat in the stillness of the room. Victoria stared at him, her eyes wide. "Yes, that's right. After I shot him, after I killed him, I took the cuff from his wrist and put it on my own. As a reminder that I'd had no choice. As a reminder of what I'd become."

He took a deep breath and continued. "In that moment I became a product of violence. My entire life from the moment after that has been driven by violence. But when your choices are taken from you all you can do is embrace them. That day created me. It created the man that I am now. And it is not who I wanted to be."

"Then be someone different," she said. As if it were so simple.

"Because it is easy? To leave the past behind? You were completely bound up in a thwarted love affair from more than a decade ago. And you dare suggest to me that I should not be affected by killing a man?"

"We have choices, Dmitri. We always have a choice."

"I had no choice. It was either his life or mine. His life for my mother's. There was no other option."

"Maybe not. But I don't think that's what really bothers you. I don't think that's what scares you now. It's what happened after."

Her words hit too close to the bone. Too close to the wound that had never really healed.

"You don't know what you're talking about."

"Don't I? As you pointed out I'm very adept at clinging to pain from my past."

"Poor Victoria. Did a man reject you and damage your self-esteem? You made daddy upset? My daddy bled out on the floor of my home, because of me. I think I have the monopoly on issues."

"You did have a choice to make then. You made the hard one."

"It is not hard to decide to save yourself."

"You didn't save yourself. All you did was allow yourself more years to keep breathing. I think you damned yourself all those years ago. Not with your actions, but with your own condemnation."

He chuckled, the sound flat and hollow in the hotel suite. "Oh, it was not my condemnation, princess. I received it from plenty of other places. My own mother, for one."

"But she isn't here. She has no power over you. Stop holding yourself prisoner," she said. "I tied you up tonight, but your hands have been tied by that leather cuff from the moment you took it off your father's body."

Rage poured through him, at the idea that he had somehow been the one to put himself in this position. "So, you blame me, too?"

"Not for your father's death. I blame you for everything

that happened since. You are not a prisoner of that day. It does not define you. You are more than that. Colvin knew it—that's why he took you out of that bar in Moscow and made you the man you are today. I know it. It's why I… It's why I love you."

"Don't say that, Victoria."

"Why not?" she asked. "It's the truth. And one of us should tell the truth."

"Why?" he asked, his voice rough. "Why would you love me?"

He shouldn't care. He should not push her for an answer, because he did not deserve the sentiment. Because he couldn't accept it. Because he couldn't return it. And yet, he felt desperate to know. Because he was certain that she was the only person ever to love him since the moment he had taken a life. And he needed to know why. It seemed more important than his next breath.

"I thought I just wanted to sleep with you, because I was attracted to you. Because you proved to me that something inside of myself that I had thought wasn't even there, not only existed, but burned bright and hot. That night when you touched me on the balcony in New Orleans…you changed something in me. But then you made me come after you. You made me choose. And after that I knew I wanted more. And every night since then I've known it, deeper and more profoundly. Because it's like this fog that's been weighing me down has been lifted. I see myself, clearly, for the first time in years. I know what I want, and I trust what I want. I want you, Dmitri. Not just for the next couple of weeks, not just for sex. I want you. You are a fighter. A champion. You are the best man I have ever known, the only one who has ever wanted me, and not simply what I could offer. That's why I love you."

Her words were everything he had ever hoped to hear,

and for one blinding second he thought about taking them. About holding them close to his chest, about holding *her* close to his chest. About allowing her to keep him.

On the heels of that thought, on the heels of that dream, he realized he never could.

Because she loved him but it wouldn't last. Because she would realize what manner of man he was, dammit all to hell, his own mother had realized that eventually. And all of the things that had happened since he pulled the trigger and ended his father's life had only taken him further away from humanity. Further away from being the kind of man that Victoria should love, the kind of man who could love her in return.

What he wanted, what he could understand was possession. To possess her, and beg her to possess him. But it wasn't the same thing as love.

He had sacrificed that part of himself long ago. And he would never, ever give of himself in that way again. Even if he had the ability. Because he knew how badly it cut when the rejection came. And for a man like him, the rejection would come. Undoubtedly.

But for a moment, it had been a wonderful fantasy to belong to her. To be connected to another person, rather than simply being adrift in a sea alone.

But it had only been a fantasy. That was all. And it was all it would ever be.

And he realized then, it wasn't being helpless he feared. It was opening himself up again, giving everything, only to have it rejected.

He could not allow it.

He could not give up that much of his control, that much of his protection. That moment of surrender in bed was all he could give. It was all he could ever give.

"No, Victoria. It is not going to happen. It can't happen."

"Why not?" she asked, standing up from the bed, naked still, her expression full of pain. Pain he had put there. Would he ever stop harming those he cared about? "It's stupid. I don't understand why this can't happen."

"Because I don't love you."

He spit the words out as if they were something distasteful, and they were. As they left his lips, it felt as though he was being stabbed in the chest. And in his head, the word *liar* echoed, loud, never-ending.

Her lower lip wobbled and she caught it in her teeth. "Oh. Well…well."

He knew he had to end this. Quickly. Decisively.

One shot, and as long as he aimed well, it would be over quickly.

This he knew from experience.

"Remember what I said to you? About using your innocence? I think we can safely say that's effectively gone. I find myself getting bored. I don't see the need to continue on."

"I don't believe you. I don't believe you really feel that way. Not about my innocence, not when you are castigating yourself over the fact that I was a virgin."

"And you are clearly still as gullible as ever. Is it really possible that you let two men trick you this completely?" The words scraped his throat raw when he spoke them, all the pain in her eyes echoing through him. And he hated himself. But there was no other way. "Look at yourself, Victoria. You're as silly now as you were when you were sixteen."

"No!" Her voice broke on the word, and it cracked something inside of him. "I am not gullible. I am not the same. You gave me… You gave me back a part of myself. Do not take it from me. You're not allowed to take it from me. How dare you? How dare you make me feel so powerful? How dare you make me feel so strong? How do you do all of that and then try to take it?"

"You gave it to yourself, sweetheart. I didn't have anything to do with it. Because I didn't give you anything. All I did was take. Your beautiful body was enough for me. And the fact that you are up for a little bit of kink? That only makes it better. But you're not the first woman I've played these kinds of games with, and you won't be the last." It was a lie. No woman had ever touched him as she had; no woman had ever bound his wrists.

No woman had ever made him feel as if he wanted to belong to her. To be hers, and nothing else.

No woman had ever got beneath his solidly built defenses, and that was why he had to send her away now.

She swallowed hard, visibly, then lifted her shaking finger and pointed toward the door. "Get out."

"This is my hotel room, princess." He couldn't bring himself to use her name anymore. He needed distance. "You're in no position to throw me out."

"You infuriating, insufferable man." She set about collecting her clothes, her entire frame shaking. "I am not a fool. Not now, not ever. I will not make myself responsible for your sins. Neither will I ever allow you to think of me as some sort of sacrificial lamb who somehow eased your trauma by giving you my so-called innocence. I gave you nothing less than what I wanted to give you. It was *my* choice. You took nothing from me. And I don't need to feel sorry about it. You should be sorry. You should be sorry. Nathan should be sorry. My father should be sorry. But I will not be sorry. I will not be sorry for loving any of you. For caring. For believing the best in people even when it came back to bite me. And I am the one breaking off this engagement."

"You can't do that." His words came out raw. "According to the agreement if you do that then you do not get the company."

"I don't want it. Not anymore. I don't want anything from you. I don't want anything for my father. I'm done paying for my mistakes. I'm done trying to be something I'm not in order to find atonement. It shouldn't be so hard to make someone love you." The sob broke the last words she spoke. "It shouldn't be this hard."

She slipped the dress back on over her curves, and zipped it up tight. Covering herself. Closing herself off.

And then without another word, Victoria Calder turned away from him, her shoulders stiff, her manner as haughty as it had been the first day she'd walked into his gym. Then she walked out of the bedroom, and he heard her walk out of the suite entirely, the door closing hard behind her.

And once again he was left alone. He wasn't out on the streets; he was still in his luxury hotel room. But somehow this was worse than when he found himself thrown out of his childhood home. Somehow, he felt more alone than he had upon realizing his father was gone. Upon realizing his mother wanted nothing more to do with him.

This was a kind of pain he'd never experienced before, the kind of pain he'd been trying to spare himself ever feeling again.

But it was too late for that. He'd imagined that because his soul was so damaged by the events of the past he had no heart left to break, no heart left to love.

But he was wrong.

He had fallen in love with Victoria. And he loved her with every torn bloody shred of the heart that was left in his chest.

The problem was, Victoria deserved more. And she knew it. Was finally asking for it.

She deserved more than a man who had nothing more than fragments left to love her with. She deserved a man who didn't have so much blood on his hands.

Someday she would realize that. And he couldn't face being with her when she did.

He put his hand on his stomach, doubling over. The pain suddenly overwhelmed him, forcing him to his knees. He had taken countless blows in the ring, countless blows in his days fighting in bars. But the pain had never been like this. If it were possible, he would tap out. But there was no escaping this.

He hadn't wanted this. He hadn't been looking for it. He had been just fine before she had stormed into his life. Proposing an engagement to benefit them both. And now she had left, gone completely, and without even allowing him to give her what she deserved.

She had left behind the company. And worse still, she had left him behind.

But it was better for her this way. Better for her to move forward unencumbered by her father and his expectations, unencumbered by him.

Victoria had spent too many years hiding in the shadows. And he would be damned if he held her back for one more moment.

Victoria was meant to shine, and he would only ever live in the darkness.

Victoria went out of her way to avoid being frivolous with her money. She did her very best to spend only what she earned from her investments, and not the money from her trust fund. Because the complicated relationship with her father had made her view that money as something not to be used. But in this instance, she hadn't cared at all. She had bought a hideously expensive ticket online, first class, back to England the moment she had walked out of the hotel in New York.

And now, only fifteen hours after she had been with Dmitri, his wrists bound, she found herself walking into her apartment in London. The air felt stale, as though no one had been there in a long time. And while it had been a couple of weeks, it certainly wasn't worthy of this feeling of flatness. Though, maybe it wasn't due to her absence, but due to the absence of Dmitri.

That thought made her angry. Very angry.

Because he did not deserve for her to feel this way about him. He did not deserve for her apartment to feel empty because he wasn't in it. He did not deserve for her chest to feel empty because he didn't love her back. She was so tired of this. So tired of loving people who were simply never going to love her in return.

You gave it to yourself, sweetheart.

His words, hard, angry, filled her with a strange sense of melancholy and an ache that she could not readily define. She wanted those words to be true. Badly. As much as she had wanted to believe that he'd given her the ability to finally be okay with herself, she also wanted to believe it had come solely from inside of herself. Because she was standing here alone, yet again, without Dmitri by her side, so the strength had to keep her upright. The strength had to remain. And she would have to be the one to sustain it.

"Buck up, Victoria. You've been through worse." Her words made a ripple in the stale air. And she knew they were a lie. Because she had absolutely not been through worse. Nathan had broken her heart, her teenage heart. Her father had done his best to keep it broken, to keep her feeling as if she'd done the wrong things.

But being with Dmitri had healed her, and broken her again.

No, he had not broken her.

Her heart, certainly. But not her. She was strong, and she was smart. The one thing she would do was learn from this. She wasn't going to spend the next sixteen years exiling herself from human emotion, from normal experiences. Wasn't going to spend the next sixteen years feeling guilty for something that wasn't entirely her fault. Even if it was her fault, she had to forgive herself. For this, for Nathan, for all of it. She couldn't spend the rest of her life hating herself, and she realized now that was exactly what she had been doing. Paying penance. She'd been using her own innocence as a means of atonement.

She was no more well adjusted than Dmitri. And all she'd done was compromise her father's fortune—it wasn't as though she had shot him.

She laughed, a rather hysterical sound. She clapped her hand over her mouth and dropped her bag to the floor, placing a second hand over the first as her shoulders began to shake. She was miserable. Miserable, and different for the first time in a long time. She was changed, and she couldn't regret it. But dammit she just wanted Dmitri, and she had to face the fact that that wasn't going to happen.

Still, she refused to let it come to nothing. She wasn't getting London Diva back for her father. And she was done making it a goal. Done trying to erase something she couldn't. Done crawling across broken glass so she could look sorry enough.

She wandered back to where she'd just discarded her bag and retrieved her mobile phone, pulling up her father's number and hitting Send before she had time to rethink.

"Hello, Dad?"

"Victoria," he said. "To what do I owe the pleasure?"

"My engagement is off," she said.

"Oh." That one word was so cold it could have restored

polar ice caps to their former glory. "I suppose I shouldn't be surprised."

"No," Victoria said, too annoyed, too sad, too changed to accept whatever he was going to say next. "No, I don't suppose you would be. Because I made a mistake once so that must mean that it's all I can ever do. But actually, the engagement is off because he doesn't love me and I deserve more."

"Victoria…"

"I've spent far too long thinking I didn't. And I've realized that I'll never be able to make the loss of London Diva up to you, and I'm not going to try anymore. Because nobody deserves to be defined by one event for their entire lives."

Her father cleared his throat. "Is that how you've felt?"

"Did you not intend for me to feel that way? Because if you didn't, let me tell you, you did a terrible job. I always assumed it was purposeful, in which case, spot on."

"There was heavy fallout…"

"Because I was taken advantage of. Because I was naive and made a bad decision. Should I pay for that forever?"

"I never intended to make you feel like you were… paying."

"But you haven't forgiven me."

There was a long pause. "I haven't forgiven myself, Victoria. For not seeing what was happening. And yes, in some ways, for how angry I was with my own daughter when… it was misdirected. I should have only ever blamed him."

Victoria's heart, what was left of it anyway, squeezed tight. "Well, maybe we should just all stop being so angry and move on. Life is hard enough without dwelling on the hardest parts."

She thought of Dmitri again and blinked back a fresh batch of tears.

"Will you come for dinner next week? I have a feeling we have a bit to discuss."

"I would like that," she said.

And even though she knew it was quite a gap to bridge, she was happy to be making inroads to crossing to the other side. Especially since her bridge to Dmitri had crumbled altogether.

"We will…be in touch about it," he said, still sounding a little too formal, a little too stiff.

Things weren't going to magically heal. But at least they'd acknowledged there was a wound.

"All right," she said.

"I do love you, Victoria," he said.

She swallowed hard, her chest tight. "I love you, too."

She hung up the phone, a feeling of relief and accomplishment battling against the loss. And she wondered why that had taken so long for her to find the courage to do.

Because it took Dmitri to make you realize you deserved it.

She walked over to her couch and sank onto it, misery rising inside of her like a tide.

She knew that in the end she would be stronger for this. Stronger for her relationship with him. Because it had changed her in important ways. Right now, she didn't feel all that much stronger. Right now, she just felt pain. Right now, she was learning that there were different levels of heartbreak. And she had not even begun to scratch the surface of it before this.

She squeezed her hands more tightly over her mouth, and felt the metal band of the ring press against her skin. She lowered her hand slowly and looked at the glittering gem. That stupid yellow diamond that now seemed so right. A ring she hadn't wanted. And now she couldn't imagine ever wearing a different one. Couldn't imagine ever wearing another man's ring, regardless of the color.

Per their agreement, he got it back at the end of all this.

She lay down on her side and pulled her knees up to her chest, still looking at the diamond on her finger. She didn't want to give it back. Because that would make it final. That would make this real. And she didn't care how much the diamond was worth, or wasn't worth. She just wanted that weight there. Wanted that sense of connection.

A sob racked her frame and she tugged the ring from her finger, holding it tightly in her palm. She would return it. Tomorrow.

And she would make the announcement about the end of their relationship, because she was not going to keep pretending. She was not going to get up on a stage in London and pretend to be a happy couple, not going to dance with him all night, not after this.

But she had forfeited her prize. So she was under no obligation.

And his charity?

She would make sure that his charity didn't suffer. Because regardless of how she felt about him right now, his charity was a good thing. And she wasn't going to do anything to compromise that. No, she would still help with that. She would just help them from a distance.

She opened up her hand and looked at the ring, resting in her palm. Yes, tomorrow she would take care of everything. Dmitri would be back in London in the late afternoon, and knowing him, he would be back in his office, or at least his gym.

His gym. He would be in his gym. Weeks of wearing suits and performing for people would have him seeking his natural environment. She knew that about him, deep in her soul.

She knew him. And he knew her.

And even though she was the one who'd tied his hands, it had held her captive, too. It had bound them together. In that moment, she'd exposed herself in a real, deep way. And he'd accepted it. And it had meant something.

It had meant everything.

"Well, maybe it didn't. Maybe it only mattered to you," she said to herself, her tone accusing.

She rolled onto her back and started formulating a plan. It was either that or drown in her tears. The plan was certainly preferable.

She would cry later. And once she started, she feared she wouldn't be able to stop.

CHAPTER THIRTEEN

DMITRI COULDN'T BREATHE ANYMORE; sweat was pouring down his face, air a toxin to his lungs that burned all the way down. He'd been punching a bag in the empty gym for hours now, the tape on his knuckles wearing away, exposing the skin beneath, wearing that away, too. But there was no solace in this, and for the first time in his life he felt that a loss. He had always been able to escape. No matter how bad things were, there had been escaping physical oblivion.

But there was no chance of escaping through sex, because he wanted no other woman besides the one he had sent away. And punishing his body in the gym wasn't cutting it either.

Because it was a punishment, because he was punishing himself. He had been from the moment his mother had thrown him out onto the Moscow streets. Why else would he have chosen to cage fight in Russian bars? Why else would he have chosen to make his fortune through pain? So that his reward would always be tempered with punishment. That was why. He hit the bag harder, his muscles screaming at him to stop, his throat and lungs on fire now. And somehow, through all of that, the part of his body that burned the most was his wrists. Where Victoria had claimed ownership. Where that leather cuff he had always worn was fastened. Like a lead weight. A shackle.

That was what Victoria had accused him of using it as.

A shackle to his past. Tying his own wrists. Letting that one day, that one moment define everything he was.

And he had. But it had to, didn't it? A sin so great his own mother hadn't been able to look at him. An act that had torn open a part of himself. A sacrifice that had been rejected…

Dear God but that rejection hurt. Still. Always.

It was the part he didn't allow himself to think about because it was easier to condemn himself than it was to dwell on that pain.

On the fact that it wasn't fair. On the fact that he had saved his mother's life and she had grieved the monster, and never once, the cost it had represented to her own child.

It cost me. I loved you. I gave you everything.

I should have let him kill me and you would have been happier.

The weight of that thought hit him like a blow and for a moment he stood there, frozen.

He had been living very much as if he had been killed that day. As if it had stolen everything he was. He had fed his body with insubstantial things. With money and women, fine food and clothes. But he had not fed his soul because he had given it up as lost.

But how could it be? How could it be when Victoria loved him?

The buzzer for the front door of the gym sounded and Dmitri stopped punching the bag, bending down to pick up a towel from the floor and wiping it across his face, his chest. He walked to the door, his chest heaving from physical exertion. If the pain in his chest hadn't been there since the moment Victoria had walked out of the hotel room, he might've thought he was having a heart attack.

He wrenched open the door and for one blinding second

he thought maybe Victoria had come back to him. But it wasn't Victoria. It was a man in a delivery uniform, holding a yellow envelope.

"Dmitri Markin?"

"Yes."

"Special delivery for you, sir."

It wasn't Victoria, so it wasn't all that special. "Thank you." It took all of his strength to manage that low-level amount of politeness.

The man inclined his head and turned and left, and Dmitri shut the door hard behind him, examining the envelope. It was blank. He tore it open and squeezed the edges, opening the top and tilting it so that the contents landed neatly in his palm.

The ring. The ring he had given to Victoria.

He swore harshly and hurled the jewelry across the room. He wanted to tear the walls down in this place, something, anything to relieve the pressure that had been building inside of him since they parted. He couldn't find any release, couldn't find any satisfaction. He had tried; it was why he had been beating his knuckles bloody for hours, why he had been pushing himself to the brink of exhaustion.

But there was nothing. Nothing to alleviate the sense of rage, the sense of helplessness, the sense of brokenness that pervaded his entire being.

He reached inside the envelope and felt a small slip of paper pressed up against the side of it. He tugged it out and turned it over, examining the neat, feminine script.

Dmitri,
Here is the ring, as promised. As per our agreement.
    Please turn on the entertainment channel at four p.m.
    Victoria

He looked up at the clock on the wall and saw that it was nearly four now. He switched on the TV, his hand shaking as he tried to use the remote to find the entertainment channel, which was certainly something he had never watched before.

There was a border running along the bottom, saying that Victoria Calder was going to speak about the ending of her engagement to Dmitri Markin. A cold feeling stole over him, in spite of how he was still sweating. She wanted him to watch this? Why? To hurt him as he had hurt her?

But she would have to know that she was capable of hurting you.

And he had done his best to ensure that she didn't know. Because what benefit would it serve if she knew that he loved her? When *hc* couldn't accept the fact that she loved him.

When he couldn't continue punishing himself if he allowed himself to have a life with her.

The time rolled over to four o'clock, and the TV screen switched over to a small studio. A petite dark-haired host sat across from Victoria, who was looking strained, but he doubted anyone else would notice. It was just that he knew her. Knew that the more serene her expression, the more pressure she was under.

The host made an introduction and then turned her focus to Victoria. "So, Ms. Calder, you said that you had a statement to make about the dissolution of your relationship with former mixed martial arts champion Dmitri Markin?"

"I do. I'm regretful over the ending of our relationship. Dmitri is a wonderful man, and I could easily see myself spending the rest of my life with him. Relationships are never simple. And sometimes no matter how badly you want something, you can't want it enough for two people."

"Are you saying you want the relationship, and he didn't?"

"That isn't really important. What is important is that I will not be able to accompany him to the final venue promoting his charity. Right now, I would find it too painful. However, I wanted to make sure that the public knew he still has my full endorsement. Dmitri's work is important. This charity is important. I truly believe that the programs that will be available in the gyms will be beneficial, and there is no other man that I would rather see heading up such a project than this one. We might not be getting married, but he has my unfailing respect. And my unending love. He is the strongest man I have ever known, and the best. And while I did come on here to make a statement about our rather unhappy news, I also wanted to make sure that I let everyone know about the Colvin Davis Foundation."

Victoria spent the next several minutes talking about the charity and letting everyone know where they could make a donation. Dmitri barely heard her. Was she acting? Was this all an act? Not her supporting the charity, for there was no reason for her to do this if she didn't care about the charity. But what he cared about was whether or not she meant that he was a good man. Whether or not she meant that she loved him.

He recognized which part of London she was in then based on the background that was visible out the windows behind herself and the host.

He picked up his black T-shirt from the ground and pulled it over his head. He should shower. He should change. But he didn't have time.

He had to get to Victoria. He had to get to her now.

Because he suddenly realized with perfect clarity that he would never be able to atone for his sins. He would only be able to ask for forgiveness. It had been easy for him to see in Victoria. The way she punished herself endlessly. That she deserved more. But he had not recognized the same thing in himself.

He did now. And he was tired of living in the darkness.

He had a choice.

He was ready to step out into the light.

Victoria felt drained after the interview. It'd been awful, sitting up there, trying to maintain composure when she just wanted to weep. When she just wanted to curl into a little ball of misery and lie on the floor for the rest of her life.

Unfortunately, there wasn't a lot of demand in the little ball of misery market. No one seemed to have much use for one, it didn't pay very well and at the end of the day, it was intensely boring.

She took a deep breath and stepped out onto the London street, putting her sunglasses on as she did. She wanted the freedom to cry a little bit as she walked back to her apartment. It wasn't that far, and it was preferable to taking a cab or the tube in her current condition.

She dodged the deep scars in the pavement as she went, thinking that she imagined it was what the inside of her chest looked like about now. Cracked. Broken.

Damn that man.

The people in front of her slowed, and she could sense that something was holding up the flow of foot traffic. She looked up and saw a man standing there, wearing a long dark coat, dark pants and…athletic shoes.

People were walking around him, doing the skillful tuck and roll, managing to maneuver their way by him without touching him. And he was facing the wrong way, holding everything up, simply standing. Simply standing and staring at her.

"Dmitri?" She hadn't meant to say his name out loud,

but she found she didn't have a whole lot of control where he was concerned.

"You told me to watch you on TV. I did. I figured out you were filming near here."

"Yes. I was." The response sounded so stupid, because it was obvious, but she couldn't come up with anything more clever.

"Did you mean what you said?"

"Of course I did. Dmitri, regardless of what went on between us it doesn't change the fact that your charity is worthy. It doesn't change the fact that what you're doing is good." She wanted him to know that. Wanted him to understand his value, because he certainly didn't seem to.

"Not that." He took an unsteady breath. "Not that."

"Then what?" Her heart was beating so fast, she was afraid it would beat right through her chest.

"Did you mean it when you said you would always love me?"

She felt light-headed now, dizzy. She had said that. She hadn't even been aware of it. It had simply come pouring out of her because it was true. "We're blocking the way."

He closed the distance between them, grabbing hold of her arms and tugging her close to him. "I don't care. People can walk around us. Did you mean it?"

"What does it matter?"

"It is everything," he said, his voice rough. "It is all that matters."

"Yes. Yes, Dmitri, it's true. I love you. I loved you when you said all of that horrible stuff to me in your hotel room. I loved you while I lay down on my couch and cried. I loved you when I took your ring off my finger and put it in that courier's envelope. And I love you now. Right now, standing here on the street, with you giving me the third degree and not telling me why."

"Thank God." He cupped the back of her head and pulled her to him, kissing her hard, kissing her deep. "Thank God for that."

She pulled away from him, anger, hope, desire all vying for top spot inside of her. "Aren't you going to tell me why?" She desperately tried to catch her breath. "You said you didn't love me."

"I lied to you. I knew I loved you, I knew I loved you when I sent you away. This is not new information to me. Victoria, I think I have loved you from the moment you chose me at that ball in New Orleans. And that night in New York when you tied my hands, when you made me yours, I wanted nothing more than to stay that way, forever. But I told myself it would end. I told myself it always did. After all, my own mother didn't want me—why would you? But I realized something else today. It wasn't that. I have been punishing myself since that day my father died. Everything I've done has kept me there, in the past. If I won, that win was always tempered by blows to the face. Literally, in most cases. Victoria, choosing passion is choosing to leave behind my sins. To do more than seek out temporary means of forgiveness. Choosing to be with you means that I can't punish myself anymore. It means I can't protect myself anymore."

"You don't need to protect yourself from me," she said.

"But I did, my love, because I knew you had the power to devastate me. I knew that day my own mother wished that I had died instead and so I…I took that on myself. I lived as though I had died that day. As though I'd lost everything I was. I let that rejection, that wound, define me. I couldn't face the idea of being rejected again."

Her throat tightened, tears stinging her eyes. "I understand, Dmitri. I understand that so well."

"I know you do. And I saw what you were doing to yourself, and yet still somehow had a blind spot in my own life."

"Because it's so much easier to see the flaws in other people than it is to see them in yourself," she said. "Certainly I recognized that you needed to change much sooner than I realized I needed to. But, Dmitri, I needed to change, too. You've changed me. You made me want more. You made me trust myself again. I hated my desires. I hated them for so long. I thought my feelings were broken, evil. But you made me see things differently. You made me see me differently."

"You've done the same for me. Because, Victoria, if you love me, how can I hate myself? And I did. For so long. I said I left the man I once was behind, but he followed me around, a constant reminder of what I did. Of how my mother hated me in the end. I couldn't let go, and so I couldn't move on. I could never have more than that horrible moment back in Moscow because I was still living in it."

"Please don't hate yourself," she said, the words coming out a choked whisper. "You are the best man that I know. I meant that, too."

"I was just a scared boy, and when my own mother looked at me like I was the devil, it was easy to believe that I was. And everything hurts so much I was constantly looking for ways to manage it, ways to deal with it while holding on to it. While keeping the reminder. That was why I fought. To remind myself that I didn't deserve life, success, without pain."

"That was why I lived life the way I did, too. Lonely. Striving to please my father. Because I didn't deserve to forget. I didn't deserve to walk away from my mistake. But I'm done with that. I realize now that your mother, my father, should've loved us. My father should've hugged me after. He should've blamed the villain. But instead he blamed his daughter. And so I was still blaming me. I'm not saying I have no fault in what happened, but don't I deserve to walk away? Haven't I paid enough at some point? Haven't you?"

"I think we both have."

"I love you, Dmitri. I want to stop living life as Geoffrey Calder's disgraced daughter. I just want to be Victoria. And with you, for the first time in so long, that's what I feel like. Just Victoria."

"Just Victoria who walked into my life like a hurricane and changed everything. You're quite something, just Victoria."

"So are you, Dmitri. So are you. Maybe neither of us are so bad. How could we be? We changed each other."

"I love you, Victoria. I left love behind the day I left my family home. I haven't loved anyone since. And I know full well no one has loved me. Until now. Until you. And I don't have room inside of me anymore for anger, for hate, hate directed at other people or myself. Because I'm too full with what I feel for you."

"Oh, Dmitri. Me, too. Me, too."

She wrapped her arms around his neck and kissed him, and she didn't care that everyone was having to walk around them. Didn't care that they were holding up traffic, didn't care that they were making a scene. Only a month ago, she wouldn't have allowed something like this. Wouldn't have let herself be in the way. Wouldn't have exposed herself to criticism in this way. But she didn't care now.

Because she was happy. Because she was in love.

Because Dmitri loved her for who she was, not for how she behaved.

He stepped away from her again, reaching into the pocket of his jacket and taking out the ring. "I want to give this to you now, again. For real."

"Oh…"

"Unless you want a clear diamond. I won't force you to wear a ring you don't want."

"It's funny. I wouldn't choose a different ring now. Because this one came from you."

"To make you angry."

"I think that makes me like it even more. I think yellow is my color, after all."

He took her hand in his and slid the ring onto her finger. So different from the first time he'd given it to her, when she had put it on her own hand. When she had been angry with him for going against what she had asked for just to be contrary. "Victoria, will you marry me? And will you allow me to give your family London Diva as a wedding present?"

She scrubbed at her face, wiped away the tears that were flowing down her cheeks. "I will. To both. But you know I don't need London Diva."

"I know. But it is customary to attempt to win the favor of one's father-in-law, is it not?"

She laughed, a shaky, watery sound. She was happy, and she was on the verge of tears. She had never felt so full of emotion in her life. And it was wonderful. "I think so. And I might be on my way to being back in his favor, too."

"He should be trying to win back yours. Like I am. I have something else for you," he said. "Something that means more than the ring." He reached into his pocket again and produced the leather cuff. "This is yours," he said. "Because you are right. I was bound up in the past. And I want to be free. The only one allowed to tie my wrists…is you."

More tears joined those that had already flowed, tracing the well-worn tracks on her cheeks. She took the cuff from him and held it out. "I don't think either of us needs this anymore, do you?"

He shook his head. "I don't. I don't need anything to tie me to the past. I'm ready to walk into the future."

She turned and tossed the cuff into the bin. "I'd love to have been more dramatic and thrown it over a bridge or something, but I don't want to spoil the moment by getting a fine for littering."

He laughed. "Well…there was slightly less drama to all that than I imagined there might be."

"It's because you've already let it go," she said. "You already had the ceremony." She put her hand on his chest. "The change already happened here."

"Yes," he said, "it did. And I thank you for that."

"You did the same for me. So I guess I owe you thanks, too. Oh, and vows. That I'll stay with you forever and ever and—"

He cut her words off with a kiss, and when they parted, he smiled down at her. And she could sense the lightness in him. Could sense that a weight had been removed from his shoulders. That there was no longer anything standing between them.

"I know I am not a prince. This might seem like a bit of a downgrade."

"Not at all. Better the devil you love, than the prince you don't, right?"

"I'm not sure about that, but I'm very glad you are."

She pressed another kiss to his lips. "We should probably get out of the sidewalk now. And find somewhere private. If I recall correctly, when I proposed to you, you asked that I take off my dress."

"I vaguely remember that."

"I know I was a bit uncooperative the first time around. But this time, I'm feeling a little more agreeable."

"Oh, never get too agreeable, Victoria. I enjoy you far too much when you put up a fight."

"Once a fighter, always a fighter."

He laughed. "Perhaps. But I'm not going to fight you."

"I'm glad to hear that. Because, you are mine now, always and forever. Unconditionally."

"You have no idea how much those words mean to me."

"I have a fair idea. Because I know how much they would mean to me."

"Then it's a good thing that you belong to me, that we belong to each other."

She looped her arm through his, and they began to walk down the street together, keeping the pace of the crowd, rather than holding it up. "Yes, we do. Always."

* * * * *

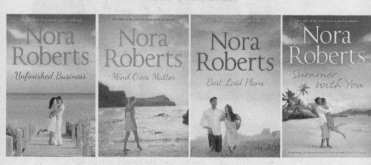

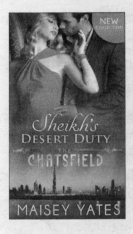